shock
point

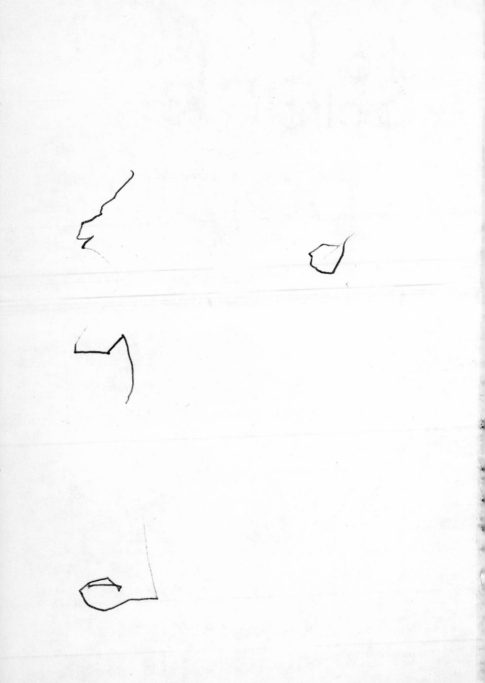

shock point

APRIL HENRY

G. P. PUTNAM'S SONS

G. P. PUTNAM'S SONS
A division of Penguin Young Readers Group. Published by The Penguin Group.
Penguin Group (USA) Inc., 375 Hudson Street, New York, NY 10014, U.S.A.
Penguin Group (Canada), 90 Eglinton Avenue East, Suite 700, Toronto, Ontario, Canada M4P 2Y3
(a division of Pearson Penguin Canada Inc.). Penguin Books Ltd, 80 Strand, London WC2R 0RL,
England. Penguin Ireland, 25 St. Stephen's Green, Dublin 2, Ireland (a division of Penguin
Books Ltd.). Penguin Group (Australia), 250 Camberwell Road, Camberwell, Victoria 3124,
Australia (a division of Pearson Australia Group Pty Ltd). Penguin Books India Pvt Ltd, 11
Community Centre, Panchsheel Park, New Delhi - 110 017, India. Penguin Group (NZ),
Cnr Airborne and Rosedale Roads, Albany, Auckland 1310, New Zealand (a division of Pearson
New Zealand Ltd). Penguin Books (South Africa) (Pty) Ltd, 24 Sturdee Avenue, Rosebank,
Johannesburg 2196, South Africa. Penguin Books Ltd, Registered Offices: 80 Strand, London
WC2R 0RL, England.

Library of Congress Cataloging-in-Publication Data
Henry, April. Shock point / by April Henry.
p. cm. Summary: Fifteen-year-old Cassie Streng is determined to expose her stepfather after
learning that he is giving a dangerous experimental drug to his teenaged psychiatric patients,
but he sends her to a boot camp for troubled teens in Mexico in order to keep her quiet.
[1. Juvenile delinquents—Rehabilitation—Fiction. 2. Camps—Fiction. 3. Psychological abuse—
Fiction. 4. Psychiatrists—Malpractice—Fiction. 5. Stepfathers—Fiction. 6. Family problems—
Fiction.] I. Title. PZ7.H39356Sho 2006 [Fic]—dc22 2005008409 ISBN 0-399-24385-2
10 9 8 7 6 5 4 3 2

This one's for Sadie.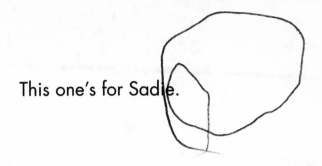

ACKNOWLEDGMENTS:

I am the luckiest author in the world, because I have Wendy Schmalz as my agent. She is tenacious, funny, and smart.

My writer pals Zeke Sinclair and Gregg Main looked at an early draft and gave me their thoughts. Gregg's daughter, Emily, read a first draft as well. Her excitement helped me know I was onto something. Then Michael Wilde helped make a good thing better.

This is my sixth book, but John Rudolph showed me what it really means to be edited. The process was truly collaborative, and *Shock Point* is a much better book as a result.

My husband and my mother have been unwavering in their support. My daughter listened to me read every word of this book aloud (sometimes many more times than once), gave me lots of feedback, and even named several of the characters.

part
one

part
one

one

April 14

It was the rough hand over her mouth that convinced Cassie Streng that what was happening was real. That and the way the other man grabbed her legs.

Five minutes earlier, Cassie had gotten off the school bus and walked up the hill toward her house. A white van was parked in her driveway. She hadn't recognized the van. She barely recognized the house—after nearly sixteen years of living in the same house, it was hard to get used to someplace you had only lived in for two months.

There was a squealing metal sound, like a door opening. Then hands grabbed her from behind. An enormous arm wrapped itself around her neck like a boa constrictor.

She swung her open backpack up and behind her, and heard the man grunt as it connected. A pen bounced off Cassie's head and a book struck her shoulder. The man tore the backpack from her and flung it on the ground, then pulled her tighter against his fat belly.

Cassie started to scream, but then his hand was over her mouth, stifling her, pressing so hard that she felt the bridge of her nose shift.

This couldn't be happening to her. Cassie managed to catch a tiny fold of skin between her front teeth. She nipped it. Hard.

"Bitch!" hissed in her ear. The hand loosened for a second. She smelled fried food when she took a shuddery frantic breath, but then the hand was clamped down again, harder.

No air, no air.

Another man ran in front of her and grabbed her ankles, easily swinging her up into the air. He was short and solid, with a dyed-black mullet.

"She's a sassy one," he said, and grinned. He was still grinning when Cassie kicked him in the face. Her shoe flew off her foot. Dropping one of Cassie's legs, he clamped a hand across his nose, which was now spurting blood. The hand across her mouth loosened. Cassie dragged another breath into her lungs, then let it out in a scream.

It wasn't as loud as she had hoped; there hadn't been enough air behind it. But surely her mother must have heard. Or the neighbors, then. One of them might be dialing 9-1-1 right now.

The men grabbed her again, no-nonsense now. The mullet-haired man lifted her other ankle and caught them both under his arm. The man behind her, the one she couldn't see, clamped his hand over her mouth again.

Holding her between them like a rolled-up carpet, the men began to maneuver her around to the back of the van. The doors were now open. Metal bars divided the front bench seat from the empty back. The floor was bare except for a rubber mat and a white five-gallon plastic bucket. An iron bar was bolted on one wall, and from it hung a two-foot-long loop of chain fastened with a metal lock.

The guy holding her legs grunted as he tried to step back and up into the van. Cassie started thrashing even harder, hoping to throw him off balance. If she could just get her feet under her!

She heard the front door bang open. Hope bloomed in her. Her mom! Cassie imagined Jackie with the phone in one hand and her stepfather Rick's gun in the other. That must have been what had taken her so long, unlocking the gun from its safe.

Her mom ran around the corner. No phone, no gun. Instead she held a suitcase in one hand. The other clutched a brochure, with a starfish on the front, to her swollen belly. Cassie almost didn't recognize Jackie. Her eyes were slits, red and swollen. Had they beaten her? Had they hurt the baby? Was her mom being kidnapped, too?

She arched her back even more frantically, managed to get her mouth free. "Mom—Mom! Help me! Mom!"

Her mom looked at Cassie, then away. Something was terribly wrong. Cassie felt like she had stepped out into the air, never noticing the staircase beneath her feet. The feeling of beginning to fall.

Behind her, cold metal clicked onto her wrists, so tight that it pinched her skin. Handcuffs. The man with the mullet let her feet go, and she fell against the man behind her.

In a strangled voice, Jackie spoke to the two men. "Wait! I don't—I don't know if this is right. Do you have to manhandle her like that?"

The man with his arm looped around Cassie's neck spoke. "They're tricky at this stage, ma'am. You can't ask them to come along quietly—because they won't. They will lie and manipulate until they've got you believing that what's up is down and what's black is white."

"Mom—what's happening?" Cassie asked in a choked whisper. "What's happening to me?"

"It's for the best, Cassie. They're going to help you." Jackie's drawn-in breath was like a sob.

"What? Mom, what are they doing? Where are you letting them take me?"

The man behind Cassie gave her shoulder a little shove. "Okay, ma'am, we need to get this show on the road." Cassie took one step, two, not resisting. Her mother handed the other one the suitcase and he threw it into the back of the van. He picked Cassie's shoe up off the lawn and threw that in, too.

She heard the front door open again, and looked over to see Rick coming out of the house. He came down the steps and put his arm around her mother. "That's right, Cassie. Just go along with these gentlemen. They're going to help you with your problems."

"I don't have any problems!" she yelled. "It's you who has the problem!"

"Cassie—I found the crystal meth in your room. Don't try to lie."

Shock stiffened her spine. "What are you talking about? I don't use drugs." She appealed to her mom. "I don't! How can you even think that?"

But instead of turning to her, her mother looked up at Rick, her brows knitting together.

"Be strong, Jackie. Would you rather see Cassie in jail—or dead? This is her only hope."

The man behind Cassie shoved her. She sprawled onto the floor of the van, vainly trying to jerk her handcuffed arms forward to break her fall. Rough hands dragged Cassie forward, and turned her so that she was sitting. They unlocked the chain and slid it through her handcuffs, then clicked it closed again. She only had eyes for her mother. Surely Jackie couldn't allow this to happen. Surely she would know whom to believe.

Instead of looking at Cassie, her mom pressed her face into Rick's neck. Absently, he patted her back, but his eyes didn't move. The last thing Cassie saw before the van doors slammed closed was her stepfather's cold stare.

two

Three days earlier—April 11

"Sure you don't want some roast beef?" Rick asked, holding aloft a slice. A drop of bloody juice landed on the white platter.

"Gross," Cassie said, pushing away her plate, even though she hadn't finished her mashed potatoes and salad. "If he's going to harass me, can I be excused?"

"Cassie!" Jackie said.

"Well, it's true. He knows I don't eat meat, but he still keeps asking."

Rick looked hurt. "I'm just worried that you're not getting enough iron. A girl your age has to worry about that. As well as the fact that not eating meat means you're not getting enough riboflavin. And there are twenty necessary amino acids, and you probably are only getting a fraction of them." As a psychiatrist, Rick had gone to medical school and liked to show off his knowledge—even if it was twenty-five years old.

"She eats cheese," Jackie said, looking back and forth between them. "And eggs. And she takes a multivitamin. I can check to make sure it has iron in it."

"I've been thinking maybe we should add something else for her health," Rick said. "Socom."

Cassie couldn't believe Rick thought she needed Socom. He

specialized in treating what were known as "troubled teens." He had enrolled many of his patients in a clinical trial for Socom, and had been amazed by the results. When the company had given him an opportunity to invest in it, he had jumped at the chance.

Jackie sat back in her chair, shaking her head. "I just don't think it's natural to put Cassie on something to change her moods."

"Natural?" Rick echoed. "What's natural? If everything was natural, we would be naked, running around on our knuckles, and eating raw roots." It was already clear that Rick wasn't a big believer in nature. He had his hair colored at a salon, his teeth were dazzlingly white, and just last month he had undergone LASIK so that he could do away with his glasses. No matter what he did, though, Cassie thought he couldn't hide the fact that he was old—at least fifty—and short. "Besides, Socom changes kids' lives, Jackie. You've seen for yourself what a difference it makes."

Her mom looked down at her plate. Her voice was soft. "You're right. It did help them. But Cassie's not really to the point that we need to put her on a drug."

"But Socom's not a drug. It's an organically occurring peptide some people are deficient in. You wouldn't deny a diabetic insulin just because it 'wasn't natural,' would you?" He leaned forward, gesturing with his fork. "It's the same with Socom. It's not much different than a multivitamin."

"But you told me there had been some problems with it."

A frown crossed Rick's face. "A few patients have been refractory, but we're already working on fine-tuning that by taking out the right-handed molecules. And that issue only affects a tiny percentage. For everyone else, Socom is making a huge difference.

Socom gives kids the piece they're missing, Jackie. It makes them whole again."

Her mom held firm. "Cassie's just adjusting, that's all. She doesn't have the kinds of problems as the kids you see in your practice. It's a big change for her—us getting married, and then moving to Portland, and the baby coming. Give her a little time and she'll be fine. You'll see."

But after dinner Jackie came to Cassie's room and begged her to try to be more cheerful around Rick. "I know it's hard," she said. With a sigh, she sat down on the edge of Cassie's bed. There were dark circles under her eyes. The doctor had told her she had to take it easy. Otherwise the baby might come too early.

From the side, her mom looked misshapen—her breasts were swollen, her belly was swollen, and even her feet, tucked into stretchy black sandals, were swollen. Although they had never talked about the exact due date, it was clear to Cassie that Jackie must already have been pregnant when she and Rick got married.

"Rick really loves you, but because of his work, he jumps to conclusions. Every day he sees kids who use drugs, who get pregnant, who drop out of school—and he worries you could end up like them. He's only trying to help."

"But I'm not like that," Cassie said. "You know that."

Her mom sighed and ran her hands through her hair, tucking the strands of her bangs behind her ears. She had short dark curly hair, the same as Cassie's. "But lately you seem to go out of your way to aggravate him. You've changed so much, Cassie. You never acted like this before."

"That's only because he's always telling me stuff, but he never listens. I thought that was what therapists did—listen."

Her mom toyed with the giant diamond ring on her left hand,

turning it around so that it looked like a plain gold wedding band. "But you're not helping, Cassie. The more you talk back, the more you roll your eyes or use that sarcastic tone of voice, the harder he comes down on you. And it just leaves me feeling stuck in the middle."

"I'll try," Cassie told her mom. Even to her own ears, it didn't sound convincing. She stayed in her room until Rick and Jackie went out for ice cream. Rick allowed Jackie a daily kid-size cone, as long as she otherwise stuck to the strict diet he had devised. As far as Rick was concerned, this baby was going to be perfect.

As soon as Cassie heard his BMW pull out of the garage, she went downstairs to the kitchen and turned on the computer. But instead of starting up, a question mark began to blink in the middle of the otherwise gray screen. Cassie didn't know what it meant, but it couldn't be good. She shut the computer off and turned it on again. The same question mark appeared. The third time, the screen stayed black.

Great. Her history paper was due tomorrow, and here it was, 8:17 P.M., and she didn't even have a way to start it. The library closed in less than an hour, and the last time she had been there, all the Internet terminals had been taken. Besides, Cassie only had an instructional license and couldn't drive on her own.

She had figured she could cobble this paper together, do a keyword search on Google, snip a bit here, a bit there, and stitch it together with a few sentences of her own. Good enough for a C, maybe a B minus.

A year ago, she would have worked on the paper for weeks, would have gotten an A. But a year ago, her mother hadn't been married to Rick, hadn't even been dating him. A year ago, Dr. Rick Wheeler had been Jackie's boss and Jackie certainly hadn't been pregnant by him. Which was so gross. Her mom was thirty-nine, way too old to be having a baby.

Everything had changed, but as far as her mom was concerned, Cassie was still supposed to be the same quiet little girl who got straight A's. And both Jackie and Rick would really be mad if Cassie got a D for turning the paper in late. Her stepfather had already had several talks with her about her lack of motivation.

Now, as Cassie stared at the blank computer screen, she thought about how one more bad grade might be all it took to get her mom to agree with Rick that she needed Socom to change her attitude and help her focus.

Cassie had better figure out a way to get this paper done, and fast. Should she call that guy, Thatcher Hedrick, from school? He had told her he worked part-time at a computer store.

She knew Thatcher a little better than most of the other kids because they had both spent a few hours after school each week working together on the yearbook. He looked kind of scary, with a pierced eyebrow and shoulder-length hair dyed dead black. But a few weeks ago he had told Cassie he wanted to be a doctor because his older sister had died of cancer. He had said it offhand, like it was no big deal, but his eyes had blinked several times.

Maybe Thatcher could fix the computer. Except what would her mom and Rick think if they came home and found her alone with a boy—even if it was just in the kitchen? Besides, there wasn't time to call him.

Rick's computer. Cassie looked over her shoulder, as if someone was watching her. Which was silly. She was completely alone. But Rick had emphasized that no one was ever to go into his office. All his patient records were kept there, and he said the government had new, strict laws about confidentiality.

Cassie looked at the digital clock on the stainless steel range. She had maybe a half hour before they would be home. She went down the hall, took a deep breath, and opened the door to Rick's office.

three

April 14

She wasn't going to let them hear her cry. Cassie promised herself that as she sat on the cold rubber mat in the back of the van. The one whose nose she had broken—at least she hoped she had broken it—was half turned in his seat, smirking at her through the bars. To gain privacy, she dropped her chin onto her chest, let her bangs cover her eyes, and turned as far away from him as the handcuffs would allow.

Her chest ached as if someone had torn out her heart. She still couldn't believe her mother had done this. For seven years, Cassie and Jackie had been on their own. "It's just us against the world, kid," her mom used to say. After Cassie's dad had moved out to be with his new girlfriend (who later became his wife), Cassie had brought all her stuffed animals to her parents' queen-size bed. For the next year, she slept next to her mother. During the day, they never talked about the nights, about how her mom had nightmares and Cassie would wake her up because she was screaming. Or worse, sobbing so hard, it sounded like something was ripping inside her.

"Better stop your bawling and get used to the new reality," the guy with the bloody nose said now. Cassie had thought she was keeping her tears a secret, but he must have seen them anyway.

Out of the corner of her eye, Cassie watched as he pinched the end of his nose and then examined his fingertips. He looked over at her again, his mouth twisted and ugly. "You really messed up my nose. I can't breathe right anymore."

"Oh, c'mon, JJ, your nose has been broken before," the fat one said. He had tattoos all up and down his arms, colorful ones that must have taken hours and hours. "You're just mad that this time it's a girl."

"Yeah, and now she's crying just like a girl." JJ turned back to her. "Don't you get it? Your parents don't want you. Looks like your mom has a new baby on the way—you know how much people like babies. A lot more than they do kids who do drugs."

"Rick's not my father. And I don't do drugs." It was stupid to appeal to them. Still, Cassie couldn't help herself.

JJ just laughed. "Oh, right. That's a new one. Marty and I will have to remember that one."

Marty acted as if he hadn't heard Cassie at all. "Once you start taking drugs, you lose all self-respect. Next thing you know, you're tricking yourself on the street, driving off with some man old enough to be your daddy."

Cassie dropped her head again. How *could* her mom have abandoned her like this? How could her mom have believed Rick? Jackie must know that Cassie didn't use drugs.

But Rick had so many horror stories. About teens gone bad, runaways who didn't come back, kids who tried heroin once and were addicts for life, who started hanging out with the wrong friends and somehow ended up living at the bus station. Rick must have scared Jackie into doing this. He'd brought them to Portland, cut them off from all their old friends, and then had gone to work on Jackie so it could be just the two of them. Them and the baby in her mom's belly.

And now it seemed he had backed up his lies by planting drugs in Cassie's room.

She had to get free and find someone who would listen to her. Cassie shifted on the floor, which wasn't softened at all by the rubber mat. When she did, she became aware of something hard in the right pocket of her jeans. Her cell phone! It was one of the tiniest models, bought by her mom as a major bribe for moving to Portland.

The two guys hadn't had time to search her before they hustled her into the van. But what good would the phone do her? With her hands behind her back, she couldn't even get it out of her pocket.

And who would Cassie call, anyway? It would take too long to explain things to her dad. Thatcher knew what was happening, so he would catch on a lot quicker, but how much could a sixteen-year-old do? The best bet would be 9-1-1, Cassie decided.

But first, Cassie had to figure out how to get her hands on the phone and a little bit of privacy. And soon, before they got to where they were going. Then the chances of them searching her would go way up. The thought of their hands on her made Cassie feel like throwing up.

She swallowed hard, hearing her mom's voice in her head. *Don't go borrowing trouble. One thing at a time.* And the first thing was the phone. She shifted so that her hands were hidden from view, then pretended to stretch her shoulders. Instead she tested the handcuffs by quickly jerking her wrists apart. They didn't budge.

Ignoring the shooting pains that resulted, Cassie wiggled her sluggish fingers. Ideally, she needed a place where she could be by herself, unobserved, for a few minutes. But how was she going to manage that?

Then she had an idea.

"I have to go to the bathroom," Cassie said.

four

April 11

Everything in Rick's office was so neat—she would have to be sure not to leave any trace. While Cassie waited for the computer to boot, she spun around in his leather chair. Only the best for Rick. She looked at his filing cabinets and thought about how he had begun to treat her like a potential patient. She wouldn't put it past him to have started a file on *her.*

Opening the top filing cabinet, Cassie looked at the tabs. *Adams, Elizabeth. Bowers, Jeremy. Candlewick, Samantha.* She recognized several of the names as being kids from Minor, but she didn't really know them. They were all older or younger than Cassie. Some of them were already out of high school. She was about to close the filing cabinet and go to the next one, where *Streng, Cassie,* might be. Then she saw a name that made her stop.

Cartright, Darren. She hadn't realized Darren had been Rick's patient. Of course, it wasn't like Rick was going to talk about it, especially after what had happened.

Darren had had black-framed glasses and thick brown hair that stuck up like an animal's pelt. Tall enough to play basketball, he was too awkward to dribble a ball, let alone make a basket. He had been in honors English and math with Cassie, but they had never really talked. Later, after everything happened, she realized he didn't really have any friends. Nobody had paid much attention to him until he leapt off the tallest building in Minor. The mailman who saw him said Darren seemed to think he could fly. He was still flapping his arms when the pavement rose up to meet him.

In the weeks just before his death, Darren had changed. In class, he started whispering to himself, so low that only the people nearest him could hear it. Cassie had asked him "What?" a couple of times, but when it was clear he hadn't been addressing her, she tried to block it out.

Death made Darren someone special, romantic. A lot of people went to his funeral, cried and hung on to each other. Candles appeared on the sidewalk—still stained with his blood—and bouquets wrapped in clear plastic, and sometimes an open can of beer, although Cassie had never heard that Darren drank. People talked about him far more than they ever had when he was alive.

Cassie surrendered to temptation and slipped out Darren's file. It was surprisingly thin. On top was a sheet labeled *Socom Informed Consent.* So Darren had been on Socom? Obviously, it hadn't worked.

The next few pages were written in Rick's distinctive handwriting, which slanted to the left, sharp narrow letters, all uppercase.

Her eye was drawn to an entry dated October 3. "Has been responding well to Socom. Moods more stable. Mother reports he is more obedient." She turned the pages, looked at the last entry.

"Patient claims that he can become a bird, and has flown over his school. Last Socom injection ten days ago. Drug's side effects are worrisome."

Cassie looked at the date. October 29, three days before Darren died. She remembered because Darren had killed himself the day after Halloween. She wasn't sure what the entry meant. If Socom was so good, why had Rick been worried about Darren being on it?

On a hunch, she looked more closely at the names in the filing cabinets. Two more of them sounded familiar. Ben Tranbarger had gone to Cassie's high school, too, but had been a senior. Carmen Hernandez had dropped out in ninth grade. Ben had drunk silver cleaner; Carmen stabbed herself in the abdomen. The newspaper interviewed experts who cautioned that media attention could prompt copycat suicides. One story said that after Ben killed himself, his mom found a clipping about Darren's death on top of his dresser.

Maybe it was copycatting. Or maybe it was only a coincidence. Crazy people went to therapy, at least that was how it was supposed to work. Even so, doctors couldn't fix everything.

But when Cassie opened the two files, she saw that both Ben and Carmen had been on Socom. And just like in Darren's file, Rick had notes about how they were starting to become delusional—and that he was taking them off Socom.

Cassie needed to show these files to someone. But if she took them and he found out—well, she didn't even want to think about how angry her stepfather would be. If only Rick had a photocopier!

Then Cassie thought of her digital camera, the one Rick had bought her to try to soften the move. She had already had a camera, a Minolta her father had given her for her fourteenth birthday. The new camera had intrigued her, even if it seemed too easy. No film to buy, no f-stops to fiddle with. "Just point and shoot," Rick had told her.

She looked at her watch. 8:44. How long did she have until they came back from Baskin-Robbins? She ran upstairs and snatched up the camera from her desk.

As she steadily turned the pages and pressed the camera's button, Cassie tried to reason with herself. Minor was a small town. Rick had been one of just two therapists who specialized in adolescents. It probably was just a coincidence that he had been the one who had treated these three teenagers.

She jumped when she heard the garage door whine. Cassie wasn't done, but she hurriedly closed the files, slid them back in the right places, turned off the light, and slipped out of the office. By the time her mom and Rick came in, Cassie was coming down the stairs, as if she had been in her room all along.

But at three o'clock in the morning, panic jolted her awake. Had she remembered to turn off Rick's computer?

five
April 14

"I have to go to the bathroom," Cassie repeated, putting her plan into motion.

Leaning forward, JJ got what looked like a broken-off car antenna from the floor by his feet. He turned and poked it through the bars. Cassie flinched as far back as she could. JJ's laugh was a bray. He prodded the white five-gallon plastic bucket closer to her.

"Use that."

She recoiled. There was no way she was even pulling her pants down in front of these guys, let alone peeing. Then she realized there was no way she could—and that maybe her idea would still work.

"How am I even supposed to get my pants down with my hands cuffed?"

JJ's sneer turned into a leer. "Stop the van, Marty, and let me get in back with her."

"Nuh-uh." Marty shook his head. "I'm not letting you handle the merchandise."

Cassie said in a meek voice, "Can't we stop at a rest area or something? I promise I won't run away."

"I've heard that one before," Marty said with something like a laugh. "I don't think so. You put up a pretty good fight when we grabbed you."

Cassie kept her eyes on the mat. For the first time she noticed the rusty-brown stains. She couldn't let herself think about what they might be. Instead, she concentrated on looking broken. "That's when I thought you were kidnappers. Now that I know this was my parents' idea, what good would it do? If I get away, they'll just send me back. My mom made it pretty clear that she doesn't"—the words stuck in her throat, and Cassie had to clear it—"that they don't want me." She looked at JJ with her chin tilted down and her eyes wide, the classic submissive pose they had learned about in biology. Dogs did it, chimps did it, even fashion models did it.

JJ was going for it, too, Cassie could tell. But then Marty shot down the idea. "Every girl we get is a lying bitch, you know that, JJ. Remember the last one? I'm not losing my job over this."

Cassie realized she didn't need to get out of the van to be alone. All she needed was them *out* of the van. "Can't you just pull over on the side of the road and give me some privacy? I'll pee in the bucket if that's what you want, but I won't do it in front of you. I don't think I could even if I tried. Then, afterward, you could dump the bucket. You don't want to smell pee the whole trip, anyway."

There was a long silence. JJ watched Marty, so Cassie did, too. It was clearly his decision.

He scratched his belly. "All right. But not until after dark. Then I'll stop on a side road. And afterward, *you* empty the bucket. And if you can't wait that long, then you're going to have to pee your pants."

"I can wait," Cassie assured him. "Thank you. I really, really appreciate it." Cassie settled back to wait and wiggle her fingers. When the time came, she would have only a few seconds to act. She didn't want to think about what they would do to her if her plan failed.

six

April 12

The next day, Cassie only went through the motions in her classes, paying just enough attention to keep from getting called on. She kept thinking about Rick's computer. When she had tiptoed down the stairs in the middle of the night, the computer had been dark. But had she left it that way—or had her stepfather discovered it was on and turned it off himself? When everyone passed forward their papers in history, she didn't even care she had nothing.

What could she do, she kept asking herself. Who could she tell? There were kids she said hi to, even people she sat with at lunch. But this called for more than that. In biology, they watched a film about cell division, but hardly anyone, including Cassie, paid attention. The guy next to her was reading a magazine article called "Tony Hawk's Pro Skater 6: The Spine-Tingling Sequel." The guy on the other side was drawing a picture of Mr. Meiner being shot in the back with an arrow. Only Thatcher, who sat in front of Cassie, seemed to have his eyes on the screen.

After class was over, Cassie hurried up to him, catching him just outside the door as he swung his backpack on one shoulder.

"Can I talk to you?" Unconsciously Cassie stood close, kept her voice low. He ducked his head to hear her. His breath smelled like coffee.

Thatcher looked curious. "Sure, what about?"

"I need your advice. It's really complicated. But nothing to do with school. And not here. Someplace more private."

He hesitated, then said, "We could go to my house after school. There's no one home until six or so."

This was taking their acquaintance forward one huge step. But where else could she turn? "Okay." Cassie nodded uncertainly and looked up at Thatcher. His eyes were a pale blue that was almost gray. She realized how close they were standing and took a step back.

"Meet me out front after seventh period, and we can walk to my house."

"All right. And, um, thanks."

Cassie ducked into the bathroom, took the little cell phone out of her pocket, and dialed. Her mom answered on the third ring.

"Hi, Mom. Um, I forgot to tell you, but we're having a meeting about the yearbook after school. So I won't be home until dinnertime." As Cassie spoke, she looked at herself in the mirror, seeing herself as if she were a stranger. Who was this too-tall girl with black curly hair, the one wearing the vintage black thrift store shirtdress, the black fishnets, and the pink Chuck Taylor All-Stars?

"That's great, honey. Maybe you can make some friends there."

"Mom!" Her mom's worries made Cassie feel pathetic. A friendless loser.

"Oh, you know what I mean, honey. You've just seemed so down lately. I know how hard it's been moving here." Her mom sighed. "Will you need me to come pick you up?"

Cassie had a moment of panic. She certainly couldn't have her mom pick her up at Thatcher's house, but she also realized she had no idea how far away he lived. "No, that's okay. I'm going to walk home with somebody."

Another sigh. "Call me if you change your mind."

After school, Cassie found Thatcher waiting across the street. He was smoking a cigarette, and had a skateboard tucked under one arm. Cassie walked over to him, and without speaking they fell into step. Cassie wondered if anyone was watching them, two losers walking off together. Then she wondered why she cared.

He held the cigarette out to her. She took a quick drag. She didn't really like to smoke—she just liked feeling like an outlaw for a second. That, and the look on Rick's face if she passed him in the hall and he caught the faint scent. It was so easy to bug him that sometimes Cassie surrendered to temptation.

"Do your folks care about you smoking?" she asked as she handed the cigarette back.

He shrugged. "These are my mom's cigarettes. I try not to smoke too much. For one thing, it's expensive. And before you say it, I know smoking causes cancer, and that it's ironic," he stressed the word *ironic*, "that we both smoke when my sister died of cancer. But after my sister got sick, my mom started smoking again, because of all the stress. Plus there's a lot of time to kill when someone's at the hospital. But my mom's going to a hypnotist next week, and if it works, I guess I won't be smoking anymore, either." He took one last drag on his cigarette and ground it out beneath his Adidas with the laces tied under the tongue. "So, what's up?"

Cassie took a deep breath. "Okay. My stepfather, Rick, is a therapist. He specializes in adolescents who need behavior modification."

"What's that supposed to mean?"

"Oh, you know, kids who skip school or start getting bad grades, who drink, who use drugs, who shoplift, who"—she was about to say "have sex," but that would be just too embarrassing—"who do other stuff."

"So he—what? Fixes them by talking to them?"

Cassie shrugged. "I thought that at first, but it seems like he just gives most of them drugs. He's been testing this one drug, Socom. That's how he and my mom met—he hired her to be his study co-ordinator. They only got married a few months ago."

"Socom? I've never heard of it." They were walking about three feet apart, taking turns glancing at one another.

"That's because it's not on the market yet. It's supposed to help kids concentrate in school, have a better attitude, and stop acting out."

"So it's like Ritalin, Prozac, and a mother's prayers combined?"

"Kind of, I guess. Rick says it makes you compliant."

"Compliant!" Thatcher stopped and stared at her. "That sounds heinous! You'd better not tell my mom about it or she'll have me on it in a minute." But he smiled as he said it, so Cassie was pretty sure he was joking. "Do you really think it could be that easy? Just give everyone a pill and they won't do bad stuff?"

"Rick says it works. He thought it was so great that he bought into the start-up company that makes the stuff. That's partly why we moved up here—to meet more investors. It's being submitted to the FDA. Rick thinks first-year sales would be over ten million dollars." They were walking past some run-down-looking apartments.

"Ten million dollars!" Thatcher said as he walked down a narrow driveway that ran next to an old, gray, two-story house. He let out a low whistle. "Some people would do almost anything for that kind of money."

seven

April 14

"Where are you taking me, anyway?" Cassie asked the two men.

"It's great. You get to go to the beach, work on your tan!" JJ sniggered, then held up a brochure. She recognized the starfish on the front. It was the same brochure her mom had been holding when they grabbed her.

He opened it and slid it through the bars until it was next to her knee. She leaned closer to read it. It began with a series of questions.

> ➤ *Does your teen struggle with basic family rules and expectations?*
> ➤ *Has your teen ever been suspended, expelled, skipped school, or had a drop in grades?*
> ➤ *Does your teen associate with a bad peer group?*
> ➤ *Has your teen lost interest in former hobbies or sports?*
> ➤ *Do you have difficulty getting your teen to do simple household chores or homework?*
> ➤ *Is your teen depressed and/or withdrawn?*
> ➤ *Does your teen have problems with authority?*
> ➤ *Do you think your teen is experimenting with drugs or alcohol?*
> ➤ *Are you concerned that your teen may be sexually active?*

> *Are your having doubts about your teen's future success and well-being?*

She found herself shaking her head.

"What's the matter?" JJ asked.

It was stupid to answer. Cassie knew she shouldn't. Still, she couldn't help it.

"I'm not like that. I don't ever get in trouble. I've never gotten anything lower than a C, and I never skip class. And I don't drink or anything like that."

Marty shook his head. "What about the drugs, Cassie? Is that part of the game plan, too? Becoming an addict?"

She straightened up, forgetting her handcuffs were fastened to a chain until it whapped her painfully in the shoulder blade. "I told you that's a lie! I don't use drugs. I certainly don't use crystal meth. I don't even know what it looks like. My stepfather must have planted something in my room to get my mom to go along with this."

Marty's expression was smug. "Every kid we take says that. It's all lies. They never did anything."

But I didn't do anything, Cassie thought. *And it is all lies.* Out loud, she said, "So is this what you guys do all day—kidnap kids?"

"It's not kidnapping if your parents arrange for us to transport you to a new school. We've got signed permission and everything. Who are we kidnapping you from?"

Cassie ignored his question. A school? That sounded more permanent. She looked down at the brochure again.

At Peaceful Cove, students are effectively influenced by Mexico's warm and simple atmosphere. Being in a foreign country is more impactful on your child, expands horizons, and creates greater

28

appreciation for home and family than any American-based program ever could.

Mexico? They were taking her to Mexico? Once they got down there, what chance would she ever have for getting back?

eight
April 12

The outside of Thatcher's house reminded Cassie of a "before" picture in one of the home fix-up magazines her mom liked. The paint was peeling, the porch was canted, and the hanging planter next to the door held nothing but a dead yellow spider plant.

Thatcher took a key ring from his pocket and opened the front door. Inside, it was crowded but cozy. A half-empty bottle of Coke sat on the wooden arm of the worn brown leather couch. An Elvis painted on black velvet sneered down at them from over an old Morris chair heaped with laundry. On the dining room table, Cassie saw scattered newspapers, two unmatched cereal bowls, half-empty coffee cups, and an open box of Apple Jacks.

Thatcher looked embarrassed. "Guess we were in kind of a hurry when we left this morning."

"Is it just you and your mom?"

"Yeah. My folks broke up after my sister died."

Cassie tried to think of something to say. "What was her name?"

"Who?"

"Your sister."

"Oh. Celeste. Short for Celestial Blue. Her eyes were darker than mine." He sighed. "Celeste's eyes were the color of the sky."

"That's a pretty name," Cassie said. "Do you have an unusual middle name, too?"

"No. Thatcher's enough. My middle name is John, same as my dad's first name. I haven't seen him since I was ten, but I still get stuck carrying around his name." He picked up a black cordless phone from its cradle. "I have to check in with my mom at work. So don't say anything. I'm not allowed to have friends over when she's not here." He didn't look at Cassie when he said this last part.

"Okay, sure." It made her feel oddly happy to hear Thatcher imply that she counted as a friend.

He dialed a phone number. "Hi, it's me. I'm home. I'm going to start on my homework now." He listened for a second. "Okay, I can do that. Do I set it on hot or warm?" There was a pause. He cleared his throat and turned his back to Cassie. "Yeah. Me, too." Cassie was pretty sure his last sentence had been in answer to his mom's saying, "I love you."

When he hung up, Cassie said, "Where does your mom work?"

"She's a supervisor at Goodwill. Sometimes she brings home the coolest stuff."

"I can see that," Cassie said. The tops of the bookshelves and windowsills were lined with unusual vases, Depression glass, pieces of wax fruit, old hats made of feathers. "It sounded like there was stuff you were supposed to do before she gets home. Am I going to be in your way?"

He shook his head. "I'm just supposed to start some wash." He stood on his tiptoes, reached into a cupboard over the refrigerator, and emerged with a can of barbecue Pringles. "Are you hungry?"

"Yeah!" Other than the kid-size ice cream cones he grudgingly allowed, Rick had banned all junk food. Now their cupboards were filled with things that Cassie wasn't even sure how to pronounce, like amaranth.

Thatcher popped the top on the Pringles can, set it in front of Cassie, then went to the freezer. "You know what barbecue chips taste best with? Chocolate ice cream." He took out a pint of Ben & Jerry's Chocolate Fudge Brownie ice cream.

Cassie made a face. "Chocolate and barbecue? That doesn't sound good at all."

"You'd eat them both separately, wouldn't you? You should try them together. It's crunchy, soft, cold, sweet, salty, fatty, and chocolatey—all seven of the essential food groups."

"If you say so."

Thatcher took the lid off the ice cream and set it next to the can of chips. "You gotta use it kind of like a dip." He demonstrated by scraping a Pringle across the surface of the ice cream, then popped the whole thing in his mouth. "Now them's good eatin'!"

Hesitantly, Cassie followed suit. Her chip broke in two, but she persevered with the two halves until each had an edge of chocolate, then gingerly took a bite. A smile broke on her face. "You're right. That is good!" For the first time in months she felt relaxed, even happy.

Thatcher straddled a chair and Cassie sat down, too, moving a coffee cup out of the way.

He said, "About that Socom stuff. It sounds really messed up. I don't think it's right to give kids drugs just to make their parents happy."

His words echoed Cassie's thoughts. "Rick has even been bugging my mom to put me on Socom."

"So is that what you wanted to talk to me about? To see if I had any ideas about how to get out of it? I guess you could stick the pill in the side of your mouth and spit it out later."

"No, my mom keeps saying she doesn't want me on it, and Rick has backed off. Besides, it's not a pill. It's an injection. You only need one every couple of weeks or something." She took a deep breath. "The reason I want to talk to you is that last night I found something strange in Rick's files."

"Are you even supposed to be looking through them?" Thatcher raised the eyebrow with the ring through it.

"I wasn't really." Cassie felt herself blush, and hoped it didn't show. "Our regular computer died, so I went into Rick's office to use the Internet. I just happened to see the names on the top of a couple of his files while I waited for his computer to boot up. Three of them were kids at my old school, kids who killed themselves. I didn't even know he was their therapist."

"Then he must not be a very good one. Isn't that why you send your kid to a shrink—to stop them from doing something that drastic?"

"Well, yeah, but that's not really what bugged me. I know I shouldn't have—but I looked in their charts. All three of them were on Socom."

"Maybe these were the kind of kids who would have killed themselves anyway." Thatcher scraped another chip across the ice cream. "I mean, there must have been a reason why they were seeing a therapist."

"Maybe. But in all three of their charts Rick had notes about how they were starting to have delusions—and that he was taking them off Socom. The thing is, none of the stories in the paper about them ever said they were on it. And they killed themselves in weird ways—but they make sense if you know what was going on in their heads."

"What do you mean?"

"Well, Darren—he was the kid I knew best. He jumped from the tallest building in Minor, where we used to live."

Thatcher shrugged one shoulder. "People kill themselves like that all the time."

"Yeah, but Rick's note said that Darren had started thinking he could fly. And Ben couldn't stop thinking about purity, and he killed himself by drinking silver cleaner. And Carmen thought she was pregnant by Satan. But I don't think she was pregnant at all. She stabbed herself in the stomach. Her mom didn't find her until eight o'clock that night, after she had bled to death on her bedroom floor."

Thatcher made a face and put down the Pringle he had been about to eat. Cassie was glad to see that she was getting through to him. "I think the first thing we should do is look Socom up on the Internet," he said, then hesitated. "Except the computer is in my room."

Her mother would never, ever have let Cassie go into a boy's bedroom. "That's okay," she said. "It's not like we're boyfriend and girlfriend or anything." She could feel her face flaming.

Thatcher ran his hand through his hair, looking uncertain. "Um, can you wait a second? I need to clean up. My room's kind of a pit."

"Sure, no problem."

He disappeared down the hall. Cassie listened to muffled thuds and doors slamming while she looked around. The kitchen counter was lined with cookie jars, all of them old looking: a hen on a nest, a carousel, a bear, a pumpkin, a mushroom, a bulldog. One wall of the dining room held long wooden plate racks filled with kitschy plates from different states.

Thatcher appeared, looking slightly out of breath. "Okay. Just promise you won't open the closet door."

Cassie drew an X over her chest. "Cross my heart and hope to die."

She followed him down the hall and into his room. There were posters on the wall of bands, only one of which she had heard of. Dresser drawers had been slammed closed, but sleeves dangled out. A cloth hamper bulged suspiciously. The bed was just sitting there, the sheets and blankets roughly pulled up.

She didn't notice the computer until Thatcher sat down at a small wooden desk.

"Wow! That's your computer? It's sleek!" It was a Macintosh with a flat screen no deeper than an inch. It looked more expensive than everything else she had seen in the house put together.

"I've been doing some part-time work at The Mac Store. They gave me a pretty good discount."

He sat down, pulled out the keyboard tray, and pressed the space bar. The screen came to life.

Thatcher went to Google, typed in *Socom,* and hit return. The first half dozen hits had something to do with Navy SEALS. But number seven read *Socom—the answer for troubled adolescents?* Thatcher clicked on the blue-underlined link, and Cassie leaned in to read over his shoulder.

SOCOM—THE ANSWER FOR TROUBLED ADOLESCENTS?

Although we have a number of products in different stages of development, after extensive research, Socom, a peptide administered by injection, has emerged as our lead product candidate. Socom is one of a new class of synthetic brain chemicals that we believe will provide a powerful new therapeutic tool in the treatment of adolescent central nervous system disorders, such as behavioral disturbances, oppositional defiant disorder, depression, "acting out," hostility, anxiety, anorexia, bulimia, and addiction.

Early preclinical animal studies demonstrated the powerful potential of Socom as a treatment for patients suffering from behavioral issues. These results have been supported by the clinical studies we have conducted on over 350 individuals to date.

As measured by standardized testing (Symptom Check List-90), after receiving three treatments, patient's test scores improved, as did their ability to concentrate and their mood as ranked both subjectively and objectively. Patients using Socom markedly lessen their participation in high-risk behavior such as smoking, drinking, premarital sex, and drug use.

Extensive testing on both animals and human patients over the last three years has demonstrated that Socom has distinct advantages:

➤ *Rapid onset of action and symptomatic relief. The initial effects of Socom are observable in the first three to five days of treatment. Peak effects occur within two to four weeks, versus four to eight weeks for currently available antidepressants (which only treat some of the symptoms for which Socom is efficacious).*

➤ *Little or no side effects. Nausea has been reported by about 5% of patients, but for most it is transient. Socom, to date, has been administered to over 350 patients, with only one patient discontinuing treatment due to side effects. This is in marked contrast to all other currently available medications, which often cause short and long-term side effects, frequently resulting in the premature discontinuation of treatment.*

We believe Socom has the potential to revolutionize the adolescent behavioral disorder market, which in 2001 was estimated to be $12.5 billion in the United States alone. We believe *that Socom, properly marketed, has the potential to become the treatment of choice for adolescent behavioral issues and to capture a substantial portion of the worldwide market after commercialization.*

"All this and it mows your lawn, too?" Thatcher turned his head to look at Cassie.

"It's too good to be true, isn't it?"

"If what this says is right, parents will be demanding that it be added to every Coke."

"But we already know what it says isn't true. Look at that part right there." Cassie tapped the screen with her fingernail. " 'Little or no side effects'! What about death? Isn't that a pretty big side effect?"

"Maybe the deaths don't count if they stopped taking Socom?" Thatcher sounded doubtful.

Cassie shook her head. "You see what it says. 'Long duration of effective action.' Even if he stopped giving it to them, they still had the drug in their system."

Thatcher tapped his fingernail against his front teeth, thinking. "What I don't understand is, how come none of the parents blame the Socom for their kids committing suicide? How come they didn't put two and two together after watching their kids take a pill?"

"But remember, Socom is a shot, not a pill. Rick gave it to kids right in his office. Maybe their parents didn't even know about it."

"But what's the incentive for him to enroll kids? Does he get paid?"

"Everybody gets paid," Cassie said. "My mom explained it to me. That's how those studies work. Kids who enroll get a hundred bucks. Rick makes a lot more."

"Wouldn't they tell their parents about the money?"

"It's cash in an envelope. I have a feeling most kids just turn around and spend it."

"But if you tell people what you found, then it might change everything." Thatcher hesitated for a moment, and then added, "Maybe you'd better act innocent. After all, you don't know anything for sure."

"Yeah," Cassie countered, "but what about all the people he's got on Socom? What if someone else starts having delusions? Or kills themselves?" She had an even worse thought. "Or what if they start hallucinating about other people? What if some kid taking Socom decides that everyone at school is an evil demon or something? It could be like Columbine. A lot of people have access to guns. Even Rick has a gun."

"Can I get a look at these files, maybe come by at a time when your parents aren't home?" He must have seen the look on Cassie's face. "Sorry—I mean your mom and stepdad."

"I can do better than that. I took pictures of the files with my digital camera."

Thatcher cuffed her lightly on the shoulder. "Get out! You didn't! That was smart!"

Cassie felt warmed by his admiration. "I didn't get everything. They came home in the middle and I had to put the files back in a hurry. But this morning I put my camera and all the cords in my backpack—but I don't know if you can download it to a Mac."

"Anything you can do on a PC, you can do on a Mac, only twice as good. Go get it."

Thatcher was right. It didn't take long before Cassie was looking over his shoulder at the photos she had taken of the records. A few seconds later he clicked the magnifying tool again and again on a permission form from Darren's file, then paged forward to look at Carmen's and Ben's. He turned in his chair, and his gaze locked with Cassie's. "Do you see what I see?"

All three of the parental consent forms had been signed with different names. But all three looked oddly the same. The same loops, the same slant, the same way of crossing the t's and dotting the i's. And what they looked like was Rick's handwriting.

Slowly, Cassie nodded. Thatcher was grinning with excitement at his discovery, but when she looked at the screen, all she felt was fear.

nine

April 14

The engine whined as it went into a lower gear. They were off the freeway, Cassie realized. It was nearly time to put her plan into action. Her breath was coming shorter. Even though it wasn't warm, sweat trickled between her shoulder blades.

The van went in a large circle, and she tipped to the side. They bumped to a stop. When Cassie tried to swallow, her mouth was dry.

"We're out in the middle of nowhere, so don't even try anything," Marty said. "There's no one to see you and nowhere to run to."

Marty and JJ climbed out of van. Their doors slammed. Footsteps crunched on the gravel and then the rear door squealed open.

Marty found the handcuff key on his overstuffed ring. Cassie stiffened when his belly pressed against her as he leaned over and opened one of the cuffs. She was in the dark, alone, with a strange man who knew he controlled her. She couldn't stop the fine tremble that washed over her, but if Marty noticed, he didn't say. She looked out past his shoulder, at the dim shape of JJ. Any thought of waving down a passing car was gone. The stars were like holes punched in black paper. They were way out in the country someplace.

Marty pushed her shoulder. "I thought you were all eager to pee, but now you're not even moving."

"I can't feel my hands." Without asking permission, she swiveled so her legs hung over the bumper, then stood up. Her arms dangled at her sides like two pieces of wood. Marty had left the cuff around her left wrist, and the other handcuff brushed against her thigh.

"Hey, hey, little girl, where you going?" JJ asked. He stepped in front of her.

"Nowhere. Just trying to get some feeling back in my arms." She didn't want to waste any of her precious private time fumbling with the phone, unable to feel the buttons.

Marty made an impatient noise. "Let's get this show on the road. You wanted to pee, so pee."

"I gotta take a leak myself," JJ said, and walked off the side of the road and into some high bushes. Cassie hoped they were poison ivy.

Marty put a meaty hand on Cassie's back. "Get in, get in. And hurry up. I'll give you two minutes to get your business taken care of, and then we're getting out of here."

She scrambled inside, her hand going to her pants pocket as soon as she heard the door slam closed. A precious few seconds ticked by while she tried to pull the phone from her pocket, but with her legs bent she couldn't tug it free. She rolled on her back, the corner of the suitcase digging painfully into her shoulder, straightened her knees, and pulled out the phone. In the dark, her still-numb finger found what she prayed was the phone's power button, then pressed it. Trying to muffle the chirp of it powering up, she pushed it hard against her abdomen and coughed.

Cassie held the phone up to her face. The power light glowed green. With clumsy fingers, she punched in 9-1-1.

"Police, fire, or medical?" a tired voice said in her ear.

"Police," Cassie whispered. The hiss of the "S" seemed to fill up the entire van.

"You'll need to speak up. I can't hear you."

She made her voice a little louder. "I'm being kidnapped. I need the police."

The woman started to answer, but her voice was drowned out by a door squealing open and then a roar of anger. Marty grabbed Cassie and yanked her forward.

ten

April 12

Cassie looked at the little clock in the corner of Thatcher's computer screen. "Uh-oh, I'd better get home." It was nearly 5:00. If she were any later, her mom would start asking questions about why the yearbook meeting had taken so long.

"I'll walk you home," Thatcher said quickly. "Wouldn't want you to get lost since you normally take the bus."

"Don't you have to do the wash?"

He shrugged. "I can start it when I get back."

"It's at least a mile. Maybe two."

"I can take my skateboard and ride back—and if you live up above the school, then it will be all downhill."

Cassie was secretly pleased. "Okay. My stepdad won't be home, thank God—but you can meet my mom if you want. Only you have to say we had a yearbook meeting."

Together, they walked out into the living room. Thatcher stuck his key ring in his pocket and tucked his skateboard under his arm while Cassie put her camera in her backpack.

"I'll say we stayed late so I could teach you how to do collages in Photoshop," Thatcher offered.

"Do you really know how to do that?"

"I can make Mrs. Husbands look like she has a duck's beak or Marilyn Monroe's body. If nothing else, I've got a future at the *Weekly World News*, altering pictures to make 'World's Largest Baby Tips Scales at Four Hundred Pounds.' "

"Or 'Fisherman Catches Six-Inch-Long Mermaid,' " Cassie offered. "I love *Weekly World News*. My favorite is 'I Was Bigfoot's Love Slave,' written by a logger. A male logger." They turned onto Beaverton-Hillsdale, and Cassie pointed up the street. "We have to go back to the school, and then turn on Sunset. We live near Stroheckers."

Thatcher raised his pierced eyebrow. "You sure you want to be hanging around with the likes of me? My mom spends all day sorting through the castoffs of people who live in your neighborhood."

"Hey, we never had any money until she married Rick. Besides, you're about the only person I know at school."

"It's tough to meet people in the middle of the school year. Why didn't they just wait till summer to move?"

Cassie paused as she realized something. "Maybe those kids dying had a lot to do with the timing. Maybe Rick wanted to get out of town before anyone figured out he was their doctor."

They turned onto Sunset and began walking up the narrow, winding hill. There were no sidewalks, so they walked facing traffic. Whenever a car passed, Thatcher took Cassie's elbow.

"So what do we do now, Thatcher?"

"Maybe we should show an adult—somebody who can do something about it."

If people found out the truth, Rick would get in trouble. Big trouble. Trouble enough that Cassie's mom might finally see Rick for what he was and get a divorce. Cassie and her mom's old duplex was rented out now, but maybe in six months Cassie would be right back where she started. With her old friends in her old town, living with her mom. The only thing that would be different would be that she would have a new baby brother.

"But who would we show it to?"

Thatcher kicked a stone into the street. "I don't know. The cops?"

"But what if the police don't believe me, or don't understand what they're looking at? They'll just think I'm some kid who doesn't get along with their mom's new husband."

Thatcher was quiet for a couple of blocks, then said, "How about a reporter? Like one of those consumer-alert people on TV."

"A reporter might be good. But maybe it's too complicated for TV. How about someone at the *Oregonian*? Papers like it when they get to break a big story."

"We'll have to be careful, though. You don't want your stepdad finding out it was you who told." He looked over at her. "What do you think he would do if he *did* find out?"

Wanting to impress Thatcher, Cassie affected a bravery she didn't feel. "What could he do? I'm his stepdaughter now. Besides, my mom would never let him do anything bad to me. She won't even let him put me on Socom."

A Honda Element went by, and Thatcher stared after it with longing. "I wish I had a car. Have you got your driver's license yet?"

"I turn sixteen in a few weeks."

"Sixteen? Sweet sixteen and never been . . ."

Kissed. Cassie completed the phrase in her head. The unspoken word hung between them. Thatcher put his skateboard down and rapidly skated away from her. He tried to execute a fancy turn, but the skateboard spurted away from him. He ran after it, grabbing the waistband of his baggy pants to hold them aloft. Panting, he loped back to her. "So when you go to take your test, don't go to Powell. If you go up there, you have to drive on I-205 *and* I-84, and they make you parallel park. Go to Sellwood instead. The lady there doesn't make you do any of that."

"I'll remember that." Cassie gestured up the hill to a two-story white house with huge white pillars in front. "That's where we're going."

"That's your house?" Thatcher's tone was incredulous. "Every time we see it, my mom goes"—he made his voice high-pitched and Southern—" 'I've come home to Tara.' "

"Don't blame me. I didn't pick it. Our old house was a duplex." As they walked up the driveway, Cassie moved slower and slower. When she spoke, she kept her voice low. "If we go to the *Oregonian*, they might lose this house. I'm not sure they can really afford it anyway." Thatcher started to open his mouth, but she hurriedly added, "I know, I know. I'm the one who said it. If we don't say anything, more kids might die. I just wish it wasn't so hard to do the right thing."

Her mother must have been watching for her, because she opened the door just as Cassie was reaching for it.

"So you decided to bring your friend home." Jackie gave Thatcher a friendly smile and reached out to shake his hand as he introduced himself. Cassie saw him noticing her mom's belly and felt herself flush.

"After the meeting ended, we were still talking about what we can do with Photoshop in the yearbook," Thatcher told her. Despite his eyebrow ring, he was the picture of innocence. "So I offered to walk Cassie home."

"Would you like to come in for some milk and cookies?"

Cassie felt herself flush. "Mom! It's not like we were having a play date or something."

Her mom cringed, and Cassie immediately felt guilty. The three of them then tried to talk at once, but Thatcher's voice came out on top. "Thanks—but I have to get home."

As they were talking, Rick pulled his silver-blue BMW convertible into the driveway and Cassie made introductions. She watched Rick's eyes take note of Thatcher's long black hair, the ring in the eyebrow, the skateboard under the arm, and the sagging pants.

"Pleased to meet you, sir," Thatcher said. To Cassie's ears, the word "sir" had a sarcastic spin. "Well, I've got to get back home. It was nice meeting you guys." He put down his skateboard. "Cassie, I'll see you in school tomorrow."

"Cassie," Rick began when Thatcher was barely out of earshot, "is that really the kind of young man you want to be associating with? Research shows that a child's friends can have a significant impact on academic standing and social labeling. You talk about wanting to fit in at school—so is that the kind of boy you really want to be associating with?"

Anything Cassie could say would just get her in trouble. She turned without speaking, walked inside, and went straight upstairs to her room. Behind her, she could hear her mom talking with Rick. She couldn't make out the words, but she recognized the tone. They were arguing—about her.

eleven

April 14

Cassie managed to scrabble back against the bars, but Marty grabbed her by the ankle and yanked. Her shirt rode up and the ribbed rubber mat caught the bumps of her spine as he pulled her forward.

Trying to keep the phone from Marty as long as possible, she stretched her arm over her head. Figuring she was already dead, Cassie screamed, "I'm in a white van on I-5 South with—"

Her feet were on the ground now, her back still on the floor of the van, and Marty was on top of her, his soft gut against her belly, his breath sour and hot. His fingers encircled her wrist, shaking her hand like a terrier snapping a rat back and forth. She managed to hold on to the phone, gripping it so hard that it cut into her fingers. Then he slammed the back of her hand against the metal wall of the van, two times, three, until her fingers finally loosened. He snatched the phone up, turned it off, then pushed himself off Cassie and threw the phone down. Raising one of his heavy boots, he stomped and stomped until she knew the phone was nothing but a million pieces of black and silver plastic. JJ had run back and now stood behind Marty. His fly and his mouth both gaped open.

Marty picked Cassie up by the shoulders and thumped the upper half of her body against the floor of the van. Her head hit the corner of her suitcase. Blood flooded her mouth when her teeth clacked down on her tongue.

"You think you're pretty clever, don't you?" Spit flecked her face. He was breathing hard. "Do you know how hard it is to trace a cell phone call?"

He dragged Cassie to her feet. Still holding her by one shoulder, he raised his other fist.

"Don't, Marty—you know they don't like it when they got marks on them."

"Oh, this won't make a mark."

The blow caught her just below the rib cage. Then Cassie was on the ground, with little broken bits of the phone pricking her face, and she couldn't breathe. The air was stuck inside her and couldn't get in or out. The pain of it made her vision go dark around the edges.

Slowly something shifted inside, loosened a tiny bit, and she sucked in a breath, coughing. Breathing hurt just as bad as the blow itself. She barely noticed when Marty and JJ grabbed her under the arms and dragged her back into the van, then locked her handcuffs in place around the chain.

For the next hour, Cassie tried not to give up hope. Maybe the police had heard what she said about a white van, and any second they would be pulled off the road. But as time crawled by and she heard no sirens, she realized it hadn't worked. All that taking a chance had bought her was the loss of her phone and both Marty and JJ being pissed at her. Except JJ didn't seem that pissed. He kept teasing Marty, telling him that he should have known that Cassie was a live wire and couldn't be trusted.

Okay. The phone was gone. Did she have anything else she could use? In the left hand pocket of her jeans was a twenty-dollar bill. She also had the keys to her house. Could she hold the two keys between her fingers and sweep them across JJ's eyes like claws? At the thought, she looked up at him. He was watching her with a slack grin, which creeped her out.

Then she realized she had a better weapon. The mini Swiss Army knife she used for a key chain! Her excitement immediately was deflated. The blade was too short, less than two inches long. Although maybe she could she use it to pick the lock? Except to do that, she would have to have her hands free.

The border. That was the only answer. Didn't you have to show papers there? When they crossed the border, she would scream, yell, attract attention. Tell them she'd been raped. Say anything that would buy time for her dad to rescue her. Once she was over the border and in Mexico, how many options would she have for getting home?

JJ leaned forward to get something from the floor. He put a small red cooler on his lap. Cassie didn't know how long they had been traveling, but it seemed like it had been dark outside the windshield for hours. He reached in, pulled out a sandwich, and tore off the plastic wrapper. The smell of tuna filled the van.

It nauseated her and made her hungry in equal measures. Her tongue felt dry and swollen, and although her mouth was watering, she couldn't work up enough spit to swallow. Even more than truly needing to pee, even more than wanting to eat, she needed something to drink.

"Tuna!" Marty said. "Why do you always get tuna? I hate that fish stink."

"Quit complaining. I got you a cheese sandwich and some of those barbecue chips you like. The kettle-cooked ones." More rustling sounds of packaging being torn open. JJ lifted a bottle from the cooler, started to untwist the cap. He looked back at Cassie.

"You thirsty? Want some lemonade?"

"Yes, please." She'd even say please to JJ if it meant she got a drink.

"I'm not giving you the bottle. You'd probably break it and slit my throat."

He pushed the neck through the bars. Eagerly, Cassie scooted as close as the chain would allow. She leaned forward and opened her mouth, ignoring their ugly laughter. She managed one swallow, two, three, although it ran down her chin and neck. JJ smiled at her and twisted the cap back on. Then he and Marty looked at each other and snickered as Cassie tried to lick the last stray drops from her chin.

A minute later, or maybe an hour, she blinked. Her eyes closed and she found it hard to open them again. She squeezed her eyes together, then tried again to open them. Her lids only fluttered up halfway. She had to lay her head down. Just for a second. Cassie tilted sideways, her thoughts beginning to blur. No wonder they had laughed. Lamb to the slaughter.

When her eyes blinked closed again, they stayed that way. The world was nothing but darkness.

twelve

April 13

Thatcher bounced up to Cassie in the cafeteria. "Come eat lunch with me. I saved you a spot."

Cassie followed him, carrying her tray with a bowl of minestrone soup, a roll, and a carton of milk. The only other people sitting at their table were a couple in the middle of hissed argument. They didn't even look up as Cassie sat down. Thatcher's lunch was spread around a crumpled brown paper bag—nacho cheese Doritos, a PayDay bar, and chocolate chip yogurt. She could just imagine what Rick would say about the way Thatcher ate.

"I did some research about suicide last night," he said, cramming some chips into his mouth. "In normal teens, the annual suicide rate is 1.5 for every 10,000 people. Okay, say the overall number of participants in the trial for Socom is what their site says on the Internet. Three hundred and fifty kids."

"And there have been three deaths out of 350," Cassie said. "Three that we know about."

"Right. One out of every 117 kids on Socom has committed suicide. Or 0.85 for every 100. Extrapolating out, that's 85 people for every 10,000. That's nearly 57 times as many as the normal rate. Fifty-seven times!" He pulled a box of malted milk balls out of his sack and offered her a handful.

Absently, Cassie took them, popping them between her teeth as she pictured the numbers in her head, multiplying and dividing them. "But these weren't normal kids."

"You can't tell me that the rate should be fifty-seven times higher just because they were already having trouble."

"But maybe it's just because the sample size is so small. Three people—that's not that many."

"What are you trying to do—argue yourself out of it? Look at the overall sample size. Three hundred and fifty is pretty big. Hell, they forecast who's going to be elected president based on sample sizes that aren't much bigger. And three kids killing themselves in a small town like Minor is a huge number. I'm surprised nobody looked at it before."

"They called them copycats."

"That's because nobody knew they were taking Socom. Only now they will. Because tomorrow after school we're going to show the files to this reporter from the *Oregonian*, Michelle Haynes. Have you read any of her articles? She worked on that series about the mental hospital."

Cassie straightened in her chair. Why had she gotten herself into this? "To—tomorrow?"

Thatcher didn't seem to notice her hesitation. "I haven't told her much, just that we might have some information about a dangerous drug in the Portland area."

"But I can't let her have the files. If my stepfather sees they're missing, he'll know right away it was me. He's capable of grounding me until I go to college. I just don't know if I should chance it."

"Just let the reporter see them once, so she'll know they're real and that they haven't been altered in any way—then she can photocopy them and you can put the files back before he's even home from his office."

"But once the reporter starts asking questions, I'll be in trouble. Rick will know it's because of me."

"Not if we do it right. We can ask her to make it sound like she's talked to a relative or friend of one of these kids who killed themselves."

"That could work," Cassie said slowly. "After all, someone probably knows that Darren was on Socom, or that Carmen or Ben were. The reporter can say that she put it together—figured out all three of them were his patients and that all three of them took Socom." She took a deep breath. "All right. Let's do it. I'll get the files tonight."

thirteen

April 15

By the time the van finally stopped, Cassie didn't care. She didn't know how long she had been knocked out by whatever had been in the lemonade, but now the misery of her own body was all-consuming. Her arms felt like blocks of wood, and it still hurt to take a deep breath. Her head ached and her mouth tasted fuzzy. Her bladder was so full that she had actually tried to wet her pants, only to find that she couldn't.

Marty got out of the van. It was daytime now. He pressed a button set into a cinder-block wall so high, she couldn't see the top of it. She heard Marty's voice, and an answering crackle. There was a metal gate set into the wall, and it rattled as it slid back. Marty got back into the van.

The van drove forward, and the gate closed behind them. Without looking at her or saying anything, Marty and JJ got out of the van. The back doors were flung open. A Hispanic security guard stood looking at Cassie. He wore a uniform that looked like it belonged to some Third World army—wrinkled, with epaulets on the shoulders. On his feet were sandals with soles made of old tires. A gun was holstered on one hip, and looking at it, she knew she was truly not in America. The worst thing was the expression in his eyes. He looked disgusted by her, as if she had really managed to wet herself. He looked at her as if she weren't even human.

Marty unlocked her handcuffs, then dragged her forward and took her by one arm. The guard took the other. Wheeling her suitcase behind him, JJ brought up the rear.

The two men's grip was so hard, Cassie knew she would have bruises the next day. It was hot and humid, but she was trembling. As the three of them walked in lock step, she looked around. They were in a barren dirt yard surrounded on three sides by twenty-foot-high cinder-block walls, painted white. The fourth side was a wire mesh fence. The sun glinted off the blades of the concertina wire looped over the top. Past the fence was the ocean, a sharp drop of a hundred or more feet down a cliff.

Ahead of her was a long, three-story white building, shaped like an L, with a flat roof. There were bars on the windows, and she thought she saw a face at one of them. A few palm trees that grew outside the wall shaded one corner of the yard.

This certainly didn't look anything like the brochure.

Wordlessly, the two men marched her ahead. The guard opened a door, and they stepped into a corridor tiled with octagonal tiles that had once been white. Cassie looked through the open door of a small room on her left and gasped. Two boys lay facedown on the floor, hands to their sides. They didn't move other than to blink. A second guard leaned against the wall with his arms crossed, watching them. He turned his head to look at Cassie, bored.

The guard opened another door and they walked into a room where an older woman sat at the smaller of two desks. She stood up when they came in. She was immensely fat, dressed in shapeless slacks and a blue and white flowered top.

"Watch out for this one, Martha. She broke JJ's nose."

"What's her name?" Martha's tone was disinterested, as if it were a normal occurrence for two men to march in a teenager who still had handcuff marks on her wrists.

"This is Cassie Streng," Marty said. "From Portland, Oregon."

Martha took a list from a drawer, and made a checkmark. Then she pulled out a three-ring binder that held three rows of checks. She quickly wrote out a check—all Cassie saw were a lot of zeros—then handed it to Marty. "Until next time, gentlemen."

"It won't be long," JJ said. "We've got a package in Arizona to pick up." He leaned closer to Cassie. His breath stirred the hair on her neck. "Maybe I'll see you later." With an effort, she kept still, only letting herself shudder when she heard the door close behind them.

Martha picked up Cassie's suitcase, grunting with exertion, then put it on the desk and zipped it open. She began to paw through the ziplock plastic bags that Cassie's mom used when packing. Seeing all her stuff—her underwear and nightgown, her books and MP3 player—here in this strange place, being examined by a strange woman, looking like courtroom exhibits in their plastic bags—made Cassie feel dizzy. Her mom had even packed a mesh bag with fins and a snorkel, as if Cassie were going to a tropical vacation paradise.

The only clothes Martha handed over were a pair of underwear and a bra. She opened Cassie's makeup bag. Inside was a brand-new set of Clinique makeup. Martha slid the mascara, blush, and eye shadow into her pants pocket. Taking a key from her pencil drawer, Martha opened a walk-in closet that was filled with suitcases. Cassie's was heaved on top.

"All right," Martha said as she opened another closet. "I'm going to issue your supplies. You keep close track of them, because if you lose them, you won't get any more. First, your towel." It

was so old, the loops had worn smooth in spots. "Your sheet."
Limp and gray. "Your uniforms." Two pairs of yellow gym shorts
and two khaki-colored blouses. "Your pajamas." A single set that
looked more like hospital scrubs, only with shorts instead of pants.
"Your water bottle—you'll need to carry it at all times. And your
toothbrush." These last two were the only things that looked new.
"Sign here, please." It seemed ridiculous to sign for clothes that
even the Goodwill back home wouldn't want, but Cassie did as
she was told.

"Wait in the intake room while I finish your paperwork."
Martha opened another door and half pushed Cassie inside. It was
a windowless room about the size of her closet at home. She
guessed it might have once been a mop cupboard, but now all it
held were two scratched metal folding chairs. Overhead, a bare
bulb dangled. There was the sound of a key turning in a lock.

Cassie suddenly realized she was alone. She had to get the knife
and the twenty-dollar bill out of her pockets and hide them somehow. After a struggle, she managed to shove her hand into her
pocket, but she couldn't feel anything. Nevertheless, she gave her
fingers the order to grasp, then pulled her hand free. The knife
clattered to the floor. A corner of the twenty-dollar bill stuck up
from her pocket, but the rest was still buried.

The door handle turned. Cassie stepped on the closed knife,
covering it with her shoe.

Martha came in. "Okay—strip and then put on your uniform."
She lowered herself heavily into the other chair.

"Strip? You mean like naked?"

Martha rolled her eyes upward. "Of course I mean like naked.
Kids come down here with all their drug paraphernalia, their cigarettes, their cell phones—I got to make sure you don't have anything hidden out."

Cassie almost jumped when the woman reached forward and pinched the jeans over her hip. Then she saw what Martha held in her hand—the twenty-dollar bill.

"You won't be needing this here," she said, and tucked the bill into the U of her top. "Do you have any piercings? Because you can't wear them here, not even in your ears. The only things you can wear here are a small cross necklace or a watch, at least until you get to Level Four." She looked speculatively at Cassie's wrist. "What kind of watch do you have, anyway?"

"Timex."

Martha grunted, obviously uninterested in Cassie's thirty-two-dollar watch. Crossing her arms, she settled back. "Come on, let's get this show on the road."

Cassie stepped backward out of her mules, careful to leave the right one in the same place, covering the knife. Her fingers fumbled with each button and zipper. Finally she stood naked, shivering despite the heat, while the woman went through the other pockets of her jeans. Finding nothing, she grunted, "You can put your bra and panties back on, then put on one of the uniforms."

Of the two shirts, she chose the one that had all its buttons. Both pairs of shorts looked worn. Just bending over to put on one pair made Cassie's bladder throb.

"Can I go to the bathroom, please?" After a beat she added, "Ma'am?"

The old woman sighed heavily. "I guess I can let you use the staff bathroom. But be quick about it."

Cassie left her shoes where they were, hiding the knife, and followed Martha. She had never been so glad to see a toilet in her life. A minute later, Martha hustled her back into the windowless room. Cassie was slipping her feet into her shoes, planning on leaning down and palming the knife, when the other woman's hand grabbed the back of her neck. Her heart leapt like a fish.

"Give me those. You won't be wearing shoes here. Only flip-flops." Martha handed her some too-big black rubber flip-flops.

Cassie slipped them on. How could she get the knife without the old woman seeing it? She picked up both shoes with one hand, trying to hide the knife with the other. A stinging slap made Cassie drop the knife and fall against the wall. Grunting, Martha bent over to pick up the knife.

"That right there is a Cat. Five. Right there," Martha said, her breath coming in huffs. "Just wait until I tell Father Gary."

"What about you taking my money? What would this Father Gary say if I told him that?" Cassie couldn't believe she had been so bold. She half expected to be slapped again.

Instead, Martha narrowed her eyes, thinking. "Neither of us says nothing, then. And you'll be thankful once you realize what you missed." She put her hand on the doorknob. "Father Gary will be here in a while to talk to you."

It was only after the door clicked closed that Cassie allowed herself to cry without making any noise.

fourteen

April 14

Before she went to bed, Cassie set her alarm for 3:00 A.M., then tucked it under her pillow. When it rang, she quickly fumbled for it, feeling like she hadn't slept at all. In her dreams she had been running down dark hallways, ducking through shadowy doorways, squeezing herself into impossibly small spaces, trying to hide from pursuers she never saw.

She rolled out of bed and grabbed a small flashlight she had taken from the kitchen junk drawer. Slowly, she turned the handle of her door. As quietly as possible, she walked down the stairs. From behind the master bedroom door, she could hear Rick's slow, rattling breaths.

As she carefully opened the office door, it let out a long, low creak. Cassie froze, but there was no sound overhead. When she closed the door, she did it more quickly, and this time it stayed silent. She thumbed on the flashlight, then opened the file cabinet and went straight to the C's.

Cartright, Darren.

A sigh escaped her. Cassie hadn't realized she had been holding her breath until she heard it let go. She had been afraid that Rick had hidden the files. But here was Darren's, in the same place as before.

She pulled out Darren's file, put it down on top of the desk. But something looked different. She opened the file up and shined the flashlight over the papers. The permission slip for the Socom trial was gone. She squinted, trying to read Rick's notes by flashlight. Even though they showed what she thought were the same dates as the ones she and Thatcher had looked at before, there was nothing, absolutely nothing about Darren being given Socom. Instead, Rick just labeled him a paranoid schizophrenic, and worried about his increasing delusions. There was even something that hadn't been there before—a brief, anguished note about his suicide.

With a sense of dawning horror, Cassie realized that Rick had re-created the truth. Cassie quickly flipped through Carmen's and Ben's files, too. Anything about Socom was gone. No study permission slips or mentions in the records.

Her legs felt as weak as cooked spaghetti. She sat down heavily in Rick's chair. Now she had no proof.

Then she remembered the digital photos on the memory card, the ones she had shown Thatcher. These would have to be enough for the reporter.

On tiptoe, Cassie ran back up the stairs, pulled open the top drawer of her dresser. In the back was the Victoria's Secret bra, the one she had bought at the mall but hadn't dared to wear yet. But when she lifted the bra up and probed inside with her finger, she touched only softness. No memory card.

She picked up the other bras and shook them, then flung them on the floor. Moving more frantically, she checked under her panties, and then unballed her socks, and tossed them all on the carpet. She was left looking at the blank wooden bottom of the drawer. The memory card was gone.

Cassie heard a noise, like the softest of chuckles. Dread froze her in place. It was all she could do to look up, but she forced herself to. Rick was standing in the open doorway, watching her.

And he was smiling.

fifteen

April 15

Finally, Cassie heard the lock click open. A man with a ruddy face, glasses, close-cropped white hair, and a potbelly came in. A white edge of beard hugged the boundary of his chin, as if he were trying to draw a line to define it from his neck. Sweat gleamed on his forehead and there were blotches under his arms. Because Martha had said she was waiting for Father Gary, Cassie had half expected some guy in a Roman collar. Instead he wore jeans and a white shirt that looked like it had started the day pressed but had quickly given up.

He said nothing, just stared at Cassie intently. As he sat down, his eyes never left her face. They were only twenty-four inches apart. Reflexively, Cassie tried to edge her chair back, but the legs were already against the wall. She didn't know where to look, so finally she looked at her clasped hands. Her watch was turned so that the face was on the inside of her wrist. Five minutes passed, seven, thirteen. Occasionally, she would look up into his dark blue eyes, but his face remained without expression. He was close enough that she could smell the sweetness of his aftershave. The fake lime-y smell made her empty stomach roil. Except for the drugged lemonade, it had been nearly twenty-four hours since she had last eaten or drunk anything, and that had been a grande mocha.

After seventeen minutes, he broke the silence. Sitting back in his chair, he folded his arms and said, "I can tell by physiological signs in your eyes that you are using crystal meth."

Cassie reared back. "What are you talking about?"

"Your pupils," he said calmly. "Drug use affects your pupils."

"I don't care what you think you see in my eyes. I have never used drugs. Never."

His smile looked like someone had propped up each side of his mouth with a stick. "That, young lady, is the kind of attitude Peaceful Cove will change."

Even though she knew it was useless, Cassie couldn't keep herself from talking back. "I don't even know what crystal meth looks like. My stepfather must have put some in my room."

He leaned forward until his snapping blue eyes were an inch from her own. "Do you want to go into OP first thing? Do you?"

Cassie came to her senses. She didn't know what OP was, but it couldn't be good. "No, sir." She looked down at her lap.

"Good. Peaceful Cove is designed to get you past your denials, your defenses, your lies. To separate you from the crutches which have allowed you to live your life only for yourself, with no thought for others. You'll find that the rules here are easy to understand— and easy to obey, once you put your mind to it. You will not leave Peaceful Cove until you are judged to be respectful, polite, and obedient enough to rejoin your family."

The whole thing seemed unreal. "Isn't this against the law? How can you hold me here against my will? Don't I have any rights?"

There was a long silence. He sat staring at her, his eyes skewering her. Finally, Father Gary said softly, "I'll let that go this time, Cassie, because no one has yet explained the rules to you. Ordinarily I'd have you in OP so fast that your head would spin. And no, it's not against the law. Your parents signed a contract with Peaceful Cove granting us forty-nine percent custody rights. And don't even think about running away. We've got armed guards and barbed wire and a two-hundred-foot drop over a cliff to stop you from doing that. The people who live in the village outside these gates are all Peaceful Cove employees—and they know that anyone who turns in an escapee gets a year's salary, on the spot. If you truly want to go home, then buckle down, be respectful, and work your way up to Level Six. Once you complete Level Six, you are free to go home."

"How long will that take?" After a second, Cassie added, "Sir," because it seemed prudent.

"That's right." He nodded approvingly. "You either call me sir or you call me Father Gary. Because we are a family here. As to how long you stay, it's entirely up to you. That's the beauty of the system. It's not determined by us, but by you."

"Can I call my mom?"

He slowly shook his head to show she was truly stupid. "Cassie, Cassie, Cassie. No, you cannot. You're here because your mother doesn't want anything to do with you."

"That's not true!"

He just looked at her. She wished she could say or do something to take the fake smile off his face.

"While you are here, you will have no contact with the outside world. Not with your family, not with your friends. There will be no TV, no Internet, no radio, no magazines, no newspapers. We want you to be able to hear us, and to hear yourself, and the only way we can do that is to turn off the noise of the outside world.

"You will be assigned a buddy. Rebecca is a Level Five. You can learn a lot from her. You are a Level One, and you will stay a Level One until you can show us that you've learned something. Once you're a Level Three, you will be allowed to call your parents, in a carefully supervised situation, of course."

"How long will that take?"

"As long as it needs to take. But you must earn your privileges. So the first thing I would work on, if I were you, is your attitude."

Cassie ground her teeth together and said nothing.

Father Gary looked at her for a long, long moment. This time she met him, eye to eye. But finally, Cassie was the one who blinked.

"We use a point system to reward positive behavior. Reward— and punishment, if that becomes necessary. There are a few simple rules." Gary held up one blunt finger. "One. No talking out of group." He held up another finger. "Two. Pay attention. Three. No newcomers talking to newcomers. Four. Do your own work."

When her chin bumped against her chest, Cassie realized Father Gary had finished talking and that she had nearly fallen asleep. She was hungry, exhausted, and had never felt more alone in her life. It was then that Cassie realized the truth. Peaceful Cove wasn't a school. It was a prison. And Rick had locked her up and thrown away the key.

sixteen
April 14

"What did your stepfather say?" Thatcher's eyes were wide. He and Cassie were standing outside West Portland High, next to a handmade poster that read, "Get your legal addictive stimulants at the student store," and listed prices for various coffee drinks.

"He just said, 'Are you looking for something?' And I swear he was smiling."

"What did you do?"

"It was totally creepy. I felt like a rabbit cornered by a wolf. Like maybe if I just stayed still long enough, he wouldn't see me. So I didn't say or do anything." Cassie shivered when she thought of how Rick had looked at her, how he had pretended to be sleepy when she could tell that he was really full of himself and his power over her. She touched Thatcher's elbow. "Since the memory card is gone, I'm hoping you made a copy on your hard drive."

Thatcher shook his head. "No. I'm sorry, I should have thought to do that. But all I did was open up the file. I didn't save it to the drive."

"Can't you recover it?"

He shook his head slowly. "Even if I could find the alias for it, it wouldn't let me open it without the original file. Which we don't have anymore." His sigh was shaky. "What do we do now? We don't have anything we can give the reporter. I guess I'll have to call her and cancel."

"No." Cassie grabbed his wrist, then dropped it when two girls walked by and stared at them. "No," she said more quietly. She had been awake for the rest of the night, thinking of what she could do, of what they could do. And of what might happen if they didn't do anything. "Not having the files and not having the photos doesn't change the facts. Three kids killed themselves, and all three of them were on Socom. If we can just convince the reporter to start asking questions, she can still find out the truth for herself. All she would have to do is talk to people in Minor—their friends, their families. Someone *must* know those kids were on Socom."

seventeen

April 15

Father Gary brought a girl about Cassie's own age into the closet, gave her his chair, and introduced her as Cassie's new "buddy," Rebecca.

Rebecca had sharp features, high cheekbones, and dirty blond hair pulled back in a French twist. She managed to make her khaki blouse look like something you might actually want to wear. There was a faint white spot right under her lower lip from a healed piercing, and an acid green smiley face was tattooed on her ankle, but aside from that, she could have been a poster child for Peaceful Cove, with a tan and perfectly white teeth.

"You are going to be part of the Respect Family," she said after Father Gary left. "That means we are sisters." She gave Cassie a cheerleader's professional smile. "Our housemother is Mother Nadine. You call the other family's mothers 'mother' as well. For example, the mother for the Dignity Family is Mother Catherine. You can never, ever call the mothers by only their first names."

The words, the ideas, the strangeness of everything were all starting to blur together, and the heat had sapped Cassie's last bit of energy. She leaned her head back against the wall, wishing she could sleep, wishing she didn't have this girl sitting in front of her, talking, talking, talking.

Rebecca snapped her fingers in front of Cassie's face. She jolted up a level of wakefulness. Forcing her eyes wide open, she shifted in her seat and crossed her legs at the knee.

"You can't cross your legs here," Rebecca rapped out.

Cassie crossed them at the ankle, then tucked them demurely under her chair.

"You can't cross your ankles, either."

Cassie uncrossed her legs and sat up straight, willing herself to be invisible, willing Rebecca to go away. She didn't know what she wanted more—to drink or to eat or to sleep. At least if she could sleep, she could dream about being someplace else.

Taking a rubber band from her wrist, Rebecca handed it to her. "And your hair can't be down—it must be pulled back. As a Level One, you can never raise your eyes. When another person approaches, bow your head. The only exceptions are the teachers and Father Gary." Cassie couldn't help but make eye contact with Rebecca when she made this point. She seemed completely serious. "Unless you have permission, you're not allowed to speak to anyone other than staff or students who are Level Three or higher. And because you're a Level One, you can't talk or sit or stand without permission. For example, if you wanted to get up, you would have to say, 'May I stand?' If you wanted to go through that doorway, you would have to say, 'May I cross?' But you can only ask Level Threes or above."

"How can I tell who's a Level Three or whatever?"

"By our shorts." Rebecca's fingers caressed the hem of her navy blue shorts. "Level One wears yellow, Level Two green, Level Three red, Level Four brown, Level Five navy blue, and Level Six gets to wear black. Once you're on Level Three, you have to tell the staff if anyone breaks a rule—or both of you get in trouble for it. At Level Four, you get privileges like snacks"—Rebecca said "snacks" the way other people said "money"—"and being allowed to wear earrings. You also get to issue consequences."

"What's a consequence?" Cassie asked, trying to make sense of everything.

"The only way you can get out of here is to earn points. One hundred points means you get to go to the next level. If you get in trouble, not only do they take away points, but you also get consequented. That means anything from having to write a five-hundred-word essay to stuff that's a lot worse. If you don't ask permission to go through a doorway, for example, you'll probably get an essay. Maybe more, depending on the person's mood."

"What if I don't ask anybody and just do something?"

"Then you'll get to spend time in OP. Trust me, you don't want to go there."

Cassie had a feeling this was the only thing she would ever trust about Rebecca. She asked the question she hadn't asked Father Gary. "What's OP? And why don't I want to go there?"

"OP stands for observation placement. Sometimes we just call it 'lying on your face.' Because that's all you do." Her smile was oddly proud. "I spent sixteen days in a row in OP once."

Cassie thought of the two boys she had seen lying on the floor, not moving except to blink. "For what?"

"I passed male authority and didn't say, 'Excuse me.' "

"Who's male authority?"

"Any man who works in the program, from Father Gary on down to the Mexican cooks. If you don't say 'Excuse me' when you pass, they'll report you to Mother Nadine, and then you'll get in trouble. And even though you always should obey male authority, watch out for Mr. Chadwick. He's one of the two American teachers here. It's better not to be alone with him, if you know what I mean."

Tears pricked at the back of Cassie's eyes, but she had already cried too many times today to cry any more. "How come he's not Father Chadwick?"

Rebecca shook her head as if Cassie were being deliberately stupid. "Because he's a teacher. Only the heads of the boy's families are known as fathers. Them and Father Gary. He founded this whole place."

"How many other kids are here?"

"More than a hundred boys and about eighty girls. All from the States. But don't even dare look at the boys. Eye contact is unauthorized nonverbal communication. You might be by a boy at a PGV or in class, but you don't look at them, you don't talk to them, and you sure as hell don't touch them." She leaned closer. "And listen. Don't you dare screw up or it reflects back on me, okay? Until you learn the rules, I will be watching everything you do. And I mean everything. And don't think just because I'm your 'buddy' that I won't turn you in if you do something wrong. Because if I don't, I can get busted, too. And there's no way I'm going back down to Level One. Not when I can get to Level Six and finally get home."

"How long have you been here?" Cassie asked.

"Two years, five months, and eighteen days," Rebecca answered without even having to think. "I was fourteen when my mom sent me here."

Cassie felt dizzy. She put one hand against the wall to steady herself. There was no way she herself could be here that long. Years and years and years? "What did you do wrong?"

"I was dating a boy who was nineteen. It was completely inappropriate. My mom was afraid I was going to get in trouble." She looked at her watch. "It's dinnertime." Cassie's stomach gave an answering growl. "You walk in behind me and you do what I do. And remember—don't talk and don't look at anyone."

Cassie picked up the tattered paper sack Martha had given her for her belongings and followed Rebecca as they walked through the now-empty office and out into the corridor. They went through several hallways and into a large room where dozens of teenagers sat in cheap white plastic patio chairs, eating from mismatched tables painted white. A wide aisle separated the girls from the boys. The only sounds in the room came from cutlery, chewing, and a loud voice issuing from a tape player on a card table next to two guards who stood with their arms crossed.

As she walked in behind Rebecca, Cassie could feel dozens of pairs of eyes flick across her, but no one looked at her directly. Then she remembered that she wasn't supposed to be looking at the other kids at all, so she looked at Rebecca's straight back instead.

After putting her belongings down in the corner where Rebecca indicated, Cassie did everything Rebecca did. She took a battered metal tray from a pile, then a piece of bread, a plastic glass filled with something bright orange, a metal spoon, and finally a chipped white china bowl into which a Mexican woman ladled soup. Cassie's stomach rumbled. Rebecca sat down at a table that had two empty places, and Cassie took the seat opposite her.

The voice on the tape player was talking about self-confidence. *"Put a smile on your face and lift your head up, and you'll soon find that your attitude has adjusted to suit your expression."*

Cassie's drink was gone in one gulp—it tasted like watery Tang—and only then did she realize that no one was getting up to get more of anything. She picked up the bread and began to eat it. There was no butter, and certainly no olive oil or sea salt, like there was in the restaurants Rick liked to go to. The bread had a strange, almost sandy texture, but she was so hungry, she didn't care. The other kids ate as eagerly, scraping their spoons against their nearly empty bowls, or running a crust of bread over the bottom to get any lingering juices. Forgetting again that she was to keep her gaze lowered, Cassie glanced around the room. Everyone seemed thin, and if this was an example of a typical meal, it was no wonder.

Her gaze stopped on one girl. Around her neck a grimy cardboard sign hung from a string. In printed black block letters, it read, "I've been in this program for three years, and I'm still pulling crap." Rebecca kicked her in the shin and Cassie looked down at her tray again.

She picked up her spoon and slid it into her bowl. It was some kind of thin soup. White grains of rice and a few slices of carrot in a greasy-looking broth. She took a spoonful, brought it up to her lips. It tasted oily and rank, but she was hungry enough to overlook the flavor. It was warm and it was food. She dipped her spoon back down in the broth. Something floated to the top. A piece of fat, white and gelatinous. She prodded it with her spoon. Lazily, it turned over. Cassie put her hand to her mouth and swallowed, hard. On the back was something short and stiff. Bristles. She felt the corners of her mouth pull down at the same time as her stomach seemed to move up, pressing higher and higher.

"What's the matter?" Rebecca hissed without looking at Cassie or even seeming to move her lips.

"I'm a vegetarian. I don't eat anything with eyes." Cassie started at the small explosions of sound around her. She realized it was muffled laughter. A girl with short strawberry blonde hair and the bluest eyes Cassie had ever seen tipped her a wink. Her expression was kind, and seeing it made Cassie nearly want to cry again.

Rebecca said, "The rule is you have to eat at least fifty percent. You don't want to end up in OP on your very first day."

By trying not to think, by eating only the broth and leaving the bristly scrap of fat, as well as a chunk of pink and white bone,

Cassie managed to eat roughly half. She wasn't really here, she told herself. It was just an accident that her body was. Her heart and soul didn't need to be touched by this place.

The rest of the day went by in a blur. It turned out that Cassie's behavior was wrong in a hundred little ways, from shifting in her seat that evening while they listened to a tape about the importance of exercise, to not keeping three feet behind the next person in line, to forgetting and making eye contact with some of the other girls. Rebecca was always next to her, whispering in Cassie's ear, chiding her, riding her, correcting her.

It was a relief to go to bed at 9:30, even though Cassie's bed turned out to be nothing but a piece of plywood bolted to the wall, with only the sheet to cover her. No pillow. The girl who had winked at her during dinner—she heard Mother Nadine call her Hayley—elaborately cleared her throat. When Cassie looked at her, Hayley made a show of rolling up her own towel to use as a pillow. Cassie followed suit. No blankets, but it was so warm that they would have provided nothing but sweaty weight. There were bars on the windows, and once she turned out the lights, their housemother locked them in for the night. There was no way to escape.

eighteen
April 13

At 3:30 P.M., Cassie and Thatcher sat waiting in the coffee shop near school. Half an hour earlier, it had been crowded with students, but most of them had left to catch one of the Tri-Met buses that stopped every few minutes across the street. It was warm outside, a beautiful spring day, but Cassie's fingers felt like ice. She curled them around a mocha, full fat, grande sized, even though she had read they had something like 400 or 500 calories. She figured she needed to keep her strength up.

A woman Cassie judged to be in her mid-thirties came ticktocking in on low-heeled pumps. She was slender, with straight blond hair pulled back in a careless bun. She wore black pants and a crisp French blue shirt with the cuffs rolled up. As she took a narrow tan notebook out of her purse, she looked around the room.

"Ms. Haynes?" Thatcher called uncertainly.

Without answering, she came over and sat at their table, tucking her long legs under her chair. Her blue eyes were framed by black-rimmed glasses. Glasses that would have made anyone else look nerdy but just made her look efficient, no-nonsense, and even more beautiful by contrast.

"All right. What's this about? Drug dealing on campus?"

Cassie looked around, hoping no one was listening. She leaned forward. "No. It's about legal drugs that aren't on the market yet. They're in the testing process, but three kids have died."

"Died?" The reporter raised one eyebrow, managing to look both skeptical and interested.

Cassie launched into an explanation of what she had found in Rick's files, as well as what he had said about Socom's side effects. Thatcher interrupted, trying to explain about the probabilities, but Cassie could tell she wasn't following.

"Why would any doctor give his patients fatal drugs?" Michelle was sitting back in her chair now, tapping the eraser end of her pencil on the table, looking dubious. "And why wouldn't someone else have figured it out?"

"For most people, the drugs work. They only make a few people have delusions. And they're working on trying to tweak it so it won't happen again. But they're covering the problems up so they can still get approval."

"What proof do you have? Your boyfriend said something about you having the files?"

Boyfriend? Cassie shot a quick glance at Thatcher, who shrugged, two spots of color burning in his cheeks.

"I looked at the files and even took pictures of them. But when I tried to get them last night to show you, they had been altered. Now there's no mention of these kids being on the drug at all. And the memory card from my digital camera is gone."

"So you've got nothing." Cassie couldn't tell if Michelle's words were a challenge or a dismissal.

"No!" The word burst out of Cassie louder than she had intended. Two people waiting at the counter turned around. She lowered her voice. "The proof is these kids. Three kids died. Three kids who were taking Socom. Three kids who were patients of Dr. Wheeler."

"And Dr. Wheeler is your—" Michelle looked at Cassie, her blue eyes expressionless.

"Stepfather."

"And how well do you get along with him?"

"What does that have to do with anything?" Thatcher said, his voice angry, but Cassie laid a hand on his arm.

"It's no secret that we don't get along that well. But that doesn't change the fact that three kids died. Three kids who had the same doctor!"

"I've written about medical research before," Michelle said. "So I know there are safeguards to prevent this kind of thing. The FDA has a bunch of hoops. Research has to be reviewed by outside monitors. The drug companies themselves have rules the doctors have to follow. If these deaths were related to this drug, then some-one should have figured it out a long time ago."

"But those things only work if everyone tells the truth," Cassie said. "What if the doctor lies to the kids about what kind of shot he's giving them? What if the doctor lies to the drug company about whether someone meets the criteria because he gets ten thousand dollars for every kid he enrolls? What if the drug com-pany doesn't look too closely because the only way they're going to make money is if the drug gets on the market?"

Thatcher played what would have been their trump card, if they still had it. "And when it comes to these three kids—the par-ent signatures were all made by the same person."

Michelle's brows drew together. "These three kids are brothers and sisters?"

"No—I don't think their families even knew each other," Cassie said. "But if you look at the parental signatures side by side, they all look the same. Like the same person signed these three differ-ent names. The letters are shaped the same way, slant the same way, have the same spiky loops. And what they look like is my stepfather's handwriting. You see, if he signed them, that may mean their parents didn't ever have to know that they were on Socom." She explained how Socom was a shot, one that lasted for weeks. "Not pills, so nobody else would have to know. And he might even have told them it was a special vitamin shot, or something else that wouldn't hurt."

Cassie and Thatcher both waited as Michelle pursed her lips and tapped her pencil against the table again. She nodded her head as if she had come to a decision. Then she snapped her notebook closed and slid it back into her purse, tucked the pen behind her ear.

Cassie felt like a trapdoor had opened in her stomach.

"Look," Michelle said, leaning forward and gesturing with her now-empty hands. "It's a given that a kid wouldn't like the new guy their mom just married. I know I didn't. But you don't have any real evidence that your stepfather is this evil guy who's killing teenagers. You say nobody but you knows these kids were on this drug. You don't have any records to back this up, and you say if I talk to the families, they may not know about it, either." Michelle picked up her bag. "Sorry, but I'm not going off on a wild goose chase. If you can get some real proof, then give me a call."

nineteen

April 30

Today was her sixteenth birthday. Underneath the table, Cassie counted on her fingers to make sure, then slowly resumed eating the rice and stale crackers that counted as breakfast. She was surrounded by two hundred strangers, all dressed alike, all chewing silently, all being watched over by two guards. Instead of her mom singing "Happy Birthday," she was listening to a PGA, a personal growth audiotape, droning on and on about proper nutrition.

"If seventy to eighty percent of the food you eat is not water rich, what you are doing is clogging your body. Eat eighty percent water-rich food. Try it for the next ten days. Watch what happens to your body. It will blow your mind."

Blow your mind? How long had they had this scratchy tape, anyway? Besides, students at Peaceful Cove were given no choice about what they ate.

In her two weeks at Peaceful Cove, Cassie had realized that a nagging hunger would now be her constant companion. The pathetic thing wasn't eating rice and stale crackers for breakfast. The pathetic thing was that she wished she could have more, but there were never any seconds.

If she had been home, she would have spent all day eating.

Blueberry pancakes in the morning, a Gardenburger, fries, and a milk shake from Burgerville at lunch, and for dinner her mom would have taken her out for a Caesar salad and a baked potato, with a stop afterward at Baskin-Robbins for a hot fudge sundae with mocha almond fudge ice cream topped with extra nuts. Her dad would have sent her a box of See's Nuts & Chews, as well as a Nordstrom gift card. And then tomorrow he would have taken her out to dinner, just the two of them. She wondered what kind of story her mother and Rick had told him.

Her birthday! The idea still seemed so strange that Cassie actually pinched herself. If only this were a dream. Then she could wake up in her room with her posters and her lime green beanbag chair, her own clothes and her own choices. Except that girl, the Cassie who had walked home with Thatcher, the Cassie who had worried about taking her driver's test and making new friends— that girl was the one who now seemed like a dream.

For the last two weeks, the real Cassie had been here, keeping her eyes down, only speaking to ask permission, gagging on the weird food, crying herself to sleep at night, but quietly, so Rebecca wouldn't hear. Reality was that Cassie was going to be stuck here for months, if not years.

Cassie had never felt so helpless or so hopeless. Or so hungry. Her spoon scraped across the now-empty bowl.

There was a nudge against her thigh. Cassie jerked, then tried to hide it. Hayley, who was sitting next to her, pressed something square into her hand. Cassie's fingers explored the serrated edges. Two soda crackers. Rebecca had warned her that you were only allowed to accept another's food if you were a Level Three or above. But this was Hayley, who wore the same Level One yellow shorts. That didn't stop Cassie from palming the crackers. She coughed,

82

reached for her water, then quickly brought up her other hand and dropped the crackers in her bowl. Luckily, Rebecca was staring down at her own food.

On Cassie's second day, Rebecca had gone over the finer points of consequences. You could be consequented for horseplay, poor sportsmanship, looking at a member of the opposite sex, frowning, talking about drinking/drugs/sex, burping, or showing an "unsatisfactory attitude." A Cat. 1 offense, such as rolling your eyes, was consequented by a modest loss of points. Further along, a Cat. 3 offense, such as swearing, cost a significant number, and might drop your score beneath your current level's threshold. In that case, you would be demoted and lose whatever privileges came with your old level. Being found with evidence that you planned to run away was a Cat. 5—the worst—rewarded with both automatic demotion to Level One and a long stretch in OP.

Rebecca hadn't covered what category food-sharing fell into, but Cassie guessed it was probably a Cat. 1. The risk seemed worth it. It was more than just two crackers—which really wouldn't do much to fill her up—but how the gesture warmed Cassie, made her feel less alone. Rebecca still had her eyes on her food, so Cassie gave Hayley a smile and was rewarded with a wink in return.

After lunch, Cassie followed the other girls from her "family" as they returned their trays and then lined up single file. Three feet apart, holding their water bottles, they walked to one of the classrooms, where they joined another family to watch a thirty-minute personal growth video—PGV—on drug abuse. They listened to PGAs at every meal, and twice a day they watched a PGV. All the audio- and videotapes were on topics like alcoholism, racism, exercise, and other subjects that were supposed to help them grow. But the audiotapes just sounded like strangely worded rants. The acting on the videos was bad, and the plot lines ridiculous. The takeaway message the students were supposed to regurgitate in a follow-up essay was always obvious—drug abuse was bad, studying was good, anger bad, self-esteem good.

Mr. Chadwick leaned against the wall at the back of the room, his arms crossed. Even though he was probably not even thirty, he had only a few wisps of hair combed across his scalp. He was also half a head shorter than Cassie. Yesterday she had seen him slap a Level One boy across the mouth, hard enough that the red finger marks hadn't faded by the time class ended.

Cassie hadn't been paying much attention to the video until it showed a teenage actress blowing out candles on a cake, celebrating her newfound sobriety. She told herself it was stupid, but it suddenly hurt to breathe. A bubble was expanding in her chest, choking her. When she blinked, hot tears spilled down her face. She dashed them away with the back of her hand.

The girl sitting next to Cassie looked at her quizzically.

"My birthday," she mouthed back, answering the unspoken question. The shades were pulled down for the videotapes, so they were camouflaged by the semi-darkness.

The other girl narrowed her eyes, clearly not understanding. "It's my birthday," Cassie whispered.

Rebecca's voice cut over the sound from the tape. "Mr. Chadwick, Mr. Chadwick. Cassie is talking!"

Mr. Chadwick flipped on the lights, then walked up and turned off the TV/VCR, the high heels of his cowboy boots clicking in the absolutely silent room. He snapped his fingers. "You there. Cassie. Come over here." He smiled at Rebecca. "Very good. Thank you for being such a concerned buddy. Ten points."

As she walked to the front of the classroom, Cassie saw that the other kids had lowered their heads to stare at their desks. This seemed like a bad sign.

"You're now on talking restriction, Cassie. The next time you are seen talking, you will be give a Cat. Three consequence and go into OP."

Keeping her eyes down, she said quietly, "Yes, sir, I will not talk anymore."

Mr. Chadwick made a sound that was not quite a laugh. "That's it. You talked. Grab your water bottle, because you are going to observation placement."

"What? That's not fair." The words shot out of Cassie before she could call them back.

"You talked again. Have it your way. You just earned yourself some more time in OP."

Cassie pressed her lips together. As slowly as possible, she walked back to get her water bottle. Her mind was scrambling, trying to find some way out of this trap. But she couldn't think of one. Protesting would just earn her even more time in OP. Mr. Chadwick was clearly in a mood, and he was going to take it out on somebody, and now that somebody was Cassie. Cassie could feel the other kids' relief. At least it wasn't them. Not today, anyway.

"Jill," Mr. Chadwick said to a blond girl who was a Level Six. "Start the tape over, have them watch it, and then have everyone start work on a five-hundred-word essay. And if you see anyone talking, you report it to me."

Mr. Chadwick grabbed Cassie's arm right above the elbow. His grip was so tight that it hurt, but Cassie didn't complain. Maybe if she were really, really quiet, it would be over faster. As he marched her down the hall, Mr. Chadwick called out, "Hector!" and a big guard came running. In the OP room, two boys lay facedown, unmoving, being watched by another guard. One of the boys had black hair bleached white at the tips.

85

"Get down," Mr. Chadwick said, and gave Cassie a little shove so that she stumbled forward. Slowly, she lowered herself to the tile floor. "Facedown," he said. She lay down on her stomach, her head turned to one side. She was about five feet away from the nearest boy. The floor was gritty and smelly, and under her cheek it was damp.

"Make sure she's down, Hector," Mr. Chadwick said.

She gasped when Hector straddled her back and sat on her butt. His weight ground her hipbones into the hard tile.

"The purpose of observation," Mr. Chadwick offered, "is to give kids a chance to think. To reflect on the choices they've made. Now, what was the wrong choice you made, Cassie?" As he asked the question, Hector picked up her left arm, and lifted it up and in, so that the back of her hand rested on the small of her back.

She tensed. There was a right answer, and a wrong answer, but she didn't know what they were. "I talked when you said not to?"

Mr. Chadwick made a sound like a buzzer. "Wrong. Show her, Hector." He lifted her arm farther, so that her hand rested on her waist. The muscles in her shoulder were stretched to the point of pain, but she didn't make a sound. The second guard, a small, thin man with a pockmarked face, looked at her and then away. "It was the way you said it," Mr. Chadwick continued. "You were being insolent. You were mocking me."

She hadn't been; she was too scared to do anything like that. Should she say anything, or should she not?

He must have given a signal to Hector, because the guard pushed her arm again, forcing it higher, up to her shoulder blade, and she realized it didn't matter what she said. "Weren't you, Cassie?" Mr. Chadwick asked tenderly, and her arm was on fire now, it was surely going to snap. The tips of her fingers were as high as the nape of her neck. She didn't want them to see her biting her lip, so she bit her tongue instead. The metallic taste of blood flooded her mouth.

"Weren't you, Cassie?" Mr. Chadwick echoed. Hector was pulling her arm from its socket. He must be dislocating it. Her eyes rolled as she tried to see if the second guard might intervene. He looked at her, his teeth sunk into his lip so hard that it had turned white, and then he turned away.

Another inch. Her body was vibrating with pain. She kicked her feet and tried to buck Hector off, but the only result was that he winched her arm even higher. Her fingertips grazed the back of her head. She was nothing; the pain was everything. And Cassie suddenly knew what Mr. Chadwick and Hector wanted. They wanted to hear her scream.

So she did.

twenty

April 14

"What are we going to do now?" Cassie asked Thatcher as they watched the reporter walk out the door of the coffee shop.

It took a long time for him to answer. Finally he shook his head and said, "I don't know."

"But if we don't do something, then more kids will die."

"I know that," he said as he got up to throw away their now-empty cups. "I just don't know what else we can do."

Cassie realized Thatcher had done a lot. He had believed her when anyone else might not even have stopped to listen, let alone to care. But she had one thing driving her that he didn't: She still saw Darren's face in her dreams, still remembered what it had been like to walk past his bloodstains on the street.

She said, "I'd better get home. But this isn't going to stop me. I'm going to figure out a way. There has to be something we can do." Across the street, the bus was pulling into the stop. "Look, there's the bus. I've got to go. I'll talk to you tomorrow, okay?"

"Okay. I'll call you tonight if I think of anything."

"Better wait until tomorrow. Don't call when my stepdad might be there."

Ten minutes later, Cassie got off the bus and walked up the hill toward her house. A white van she didn't recognize was parked in the driveway.

twenty-one

April 30

Cassie spent the rest of her first day in OP trying not to cry because it just made the floor even more disgusting. The throbbing in her left shoulder went up her neck and into her jaw, and her tongue was swollen where she had bit it. Hector had left with Mr. Chadwick, and the other guard was silent, except for every two hours, when he told them in heavily accented English that it was okay to sit up and drink water. At the first break, Cassie prodded her shoulder, moving it back and forth. It still felt like it was on fire, but nothing seemed out of place or broken.

She hadn't heard the guard coming up behind her, and she let out a gasp when he pressed something into her palm. "What are they?" she asked, looking at the two small white pills.

"You take," he said, nodding his head exaggeratedly. "Feel better." She looked at his narrow, pockmarked face, trying to decide if he was telling the truth.

The boy with the white-tipped hair said, "Go ahead. They make you sleep. That's the best thing to do here." The other boy nodded, then looked away.

With a gulp from her water bottle, Cassie swallowed the pills, only half wondering what they were.

Suddenly, footsteps echoed in the corridor. The guard quickly stepped back against the wall and clapped his hands. "Everybody resume position."

Picking a spot that looked drier, Cassie stretched out on the floor. The world grew fuzzy at the edges. She closed her eyes, welcoming sleep. In her dreams she saw her mother holding a baby, but she couldn't get close enough to see its face. Thatcher whispered to her, his face contorted with urgency, but she couldn't make out the words. And then she was picking her way down the face of the cliff below Peaceful Cove, finding handholds and toeholds, when a rock loosened in her hand and she cartwheeled backward, free-falling. Cassie's eyelids flickered open for a few seconds, but then she was pulled down again into something that was more than sleep.

At the next break, she wouldn't have bothered to get up, except that the guard shook her good shoulder. "Not good sleep so long."

The boy who had talked to her earlier helped her to her feet and then looked closely at her face. "Man, Eduardo, her eyes are like pinpricks." He and the guard exchanged looks. Cassie was too blurred by whatever Eduardo had given her to care. Even now that she was on her feet, it was as if she were watching a movie, one that had nothing to do with her.

As their break was ending, a man Cassie recognized as Father Willy, one of the housefathers, came into the room. He stood over the blond boy, his hands fisted on his hips.

"If you truly tell me you are sorry, Joshua, then you shall be allowed to come back to the Dignity Family."

Joshua, who hadn't made a single sound since Cassie had arrived, began to blubber. "I am sorry. I'm truly, truly sorry." He crawled forward and began kissing Father Willy's scuffed shoes.

"That is enough," Father Willy said, stepping backward with alacrity. "Your apology is accepted."

Joshua left so fast that Eduardo had to call him back for his water bottle. Cassie slipped again into the river of sleep, welcoming the feeling of it closing over her.

Miguel, the new guard who came on in the midafternoon, tried to find ways to alleviate his own boredom. Every few minutes he would accuse one of them of moving, sometimes accompanying his accusation with a kick. In this way, Cassie learned that the other boy's name was Ryan. After an hour or two of this, Miguel called out, "Fitness!" Ryan got to his feet, so Cassie did, too. Miguel ordered them to do jumping jacks, with only thirty-second breaks in between groups of fifty, then sit-ups and push-ups. Following Ryan's lead, Cassie did them as sloppily as she could. Even so, her clothes were sopping wet with sweat by the end.

Not long after that, one of the women who worked in the cafeteria brought in tortillas and refilled their water bottles. Since there had been no lunch, Cassie and Ryan fell on the tortillas like starving dogs. Miguel said he had to go to the toilet and told the cafeteria woman to watch them. Once he left the room, she looked both ways before slipping them each a piece of yellow cheese from her apron pocket. But in a few seconds it was gone, and Miguel was back.

In the late afternoon, another person was dragged in by Hector, Mr. Chadwick prancing behind. It was Hayley. Hector had both fists clenched in her short red-gold hair. Her mouth was pulled open in pain. The cords stood out in her neck as she scrambled forward, trying to keep her weight off her hair, but she didn't make a sound. Hector lunged forward, and Hayley's face skidded into the floor.

Then Miguel barked, "Head to the right, Hayley. The rest of you, too!" Cassie was ashamed of how fast she whipped her head to the other side, how still she lay, how afraid she was that Hector might turn his attentions on her instead of Hayley.

She tried to hide her shaking at the tick-tock sound of Mr. Chadwick slowly walking around her. A pair of snakeskin cowboy boots appeared in front of her nose. One of the pointed toes poked her in the side. "Cassie, I'm here to see if you are remorseful."

She started to lever herself up on her elbows, but he put his boot between her shoulders, pressing her back down to the floor while her shoulder screamed in protest. Cassie gritted her teeth. She would say what they wanted, but they couldn't touch her on the inside.

"I really, really am sorry, Mr. Chadwick. I promise to abide by your orders in the future."

" 'Abide,' " he echoed in a mocking voice. " 'Abide.' Do you think this is some kind of advanced-placement English class? You could just say obey, Cassie. That would be simpler. Step out of your image and stop manipulating. I want you to think about that until I come back." With that, he turned on his stacked heels and walked out the door. She could hear Hector's heavy footsteps following.

Cassie was afraid to look at Hayley until Miguel called for a break. When they sat up, blood was still leaking from the corner of Hayley's swollen lips, and her chin looked like raw meat, but she managed to smile at Cassie. Her freckles stood out on her pale skin like drops of paint on a white canvas.

"No talking!" Miguel barked, even though neither of them had said anything yet. So they kept silent, but all the same Cassie felt like they were having a conversation.

As night fell, Cassie learned that kids in OP were allowed to curl up and sleep, each of them in a separate corner, but the bright electric light stayed on. Earlier, under the influence of the drugs, she had slept so much that now it seemed impossible. Her bones ached as if she had the flu. She lay facing Hayley, who was also awake. Miguel had tipped his chair back against the wall, chin on his chest, so Cassie kept looking into Hayley's eyes. Normally, she could never have looked at anyone so long without needing to look away, but Peaceful Cove was not normal, so she stared into Hayley's eyes without feeling anxious or embarrassed. Cassie blinked more and more slowly, and then, it seemed, not at all. After long minutes, or hours, or even days, something shifted. Hayley's face morphed into a butterfly, then an elaborate harlequin mask, then transformed into liquid gold, then melted away into a geometric shape. Cassie felt like she was sitting back inside her head, observing it all as if it were happening to someone else. After a while, she must have slept, although she didn't remember closing her eyes.

Sometime in the long night they got a new guard. Hayley knew him and started joking with him in Spanish. He let Cassie and Hayley move a little closer together and talk softly in English.

"Is it okay?" Cassie kept her voice low and only indicated the guard with her eyes.

"Cesar? He's cool. He started here about the same time I did."

"Only for him it's a job," Cassie said miserably. "For you, it's your life."

"No, it's not," Hayley said seriously. "This isn't my real life. You can't think about Peaceful Cove like that or you would go crazy."

"So—what?—you act like it's a dream or something?" Cassie rotated her shoulder back and forth, trying to ease the stiffness.

"Not a dream. A game. It's like a video game, one with all these levels most people don't even know about."

It sounded like a crazy idea, but no crazier than what was really happening here. "How do you score points?"

"Every time you break a rule and you don't get caught. Or every time you do get caught but you don't cry." Hayley wiped her mouth with the back of her hand, leaving rusty-brown marks on her skin.

"But can't you get out faster by following the rules?"

"That's a game, too. You can't really get out unless they want you to, or unless you get lucky and your parents realize what's going on and pull you out. It's like in school, when they try to tell you that anyone can be on student council, but then only the popular kids get elected. Why do you think hardly anyone makes it to Level Six? Think about it. Where are the incentives for the school? I know I'm not going to get out until I'm eighteen—so that gives me a lot more freedom than the rest of these kids, the ones who think that following the rules is really going to get them someplace."

"Why don't parents know what's going on?"

"Because they tell them in advance how you'll lie to them. They even let you write what you want to, but it doesn't make any difference. 'Mom, get me out of here. Dad, it's terrible. Mom, they beat me. The food is awful and has bones in it. Mom, it's nothing like the brochure.' But what they do, see, is give your parents a handbook about how you will try to manipulate them. And it explains the different stages you go through. First, denial—'I don't belong here.' Then the guilt trip—'You don't know how terrible it is here, or you would get me out.' Next, anger. 'You'll wish you had never done this to me.' And last, negotiation. 'If you bring me home, I promise there won't be any more problems.' The Stateside rep has already warned them that you'll say anything to manipulate them, that you'll twist things and lie. They've got it all figured out. And if the graduates complain, they have a whole PR department to explain how they are troubled drug addicts and petty thieves who still haven't learned to take responsibility for their own actions."

At first, Cassie had trouble placing the emotion in Hayley's voice. And then she finally did. It was a twisted kind of admiration.

Cassie must have closed her eyes then and slept, because the next thing she knew it was morning again. For breakfast, each of them got more tortillas and four tiny bananas no bigger than their fingers. Over the next few days, Cassie was deemed unrepentant by Mr. Chadwick, Ryan was judged worthy to leave, and another boy and girl were dragged in. Playing by Hayley's rules, Cassie and Hayley took turns deflecting the guard's attention, passing each other bits of food, and exchanging smiles or winks when his back was turned. Hayley got caught once and earned another three days in OP. Cassie opened her mouth to protest, but Hayley gave her a look and she didn't say anything.

"Fitness!" Miguel yelled on Cassie's last day in OP. He reached up and cranked the window closed. She knew the drill now, and with the rest she clambered to her feet. "We start with jumping jacks."

The new girl—Chelsea—didn't seem to know what she was in for. She snapped her legs and arms out straight for each one. She didn't know they were going to do at least 300, or maybe 500, depending on Miguel's mood. After 100, they got a 30-second break. Cassie drank so fast that water ran out of her mouth and down her neck, where it mingled with the sweat that had already soaked through her shirt. By now, she could smell herself. Steam clouded the window until condensation rolled down it like rain.

When the jumping jacks were over, Chelsea stood with her head drooping, her hands on her knees, her breath huffing in and out of her mouth.

"All right! Down on the floor. It's time for sit-ups! One, two, three . . ." At 50, they got another 30-second break. Cassie tried to distract herself. If you thought about it, if you thought about what was happening now and what would happen soon, you would go crazy. The break went by so fast, and then it was time for another 50, another break, another 50, until they finally had made it up to 200. Yesterday, just for fun, Miguel had pretended that the last set had really put them up only to 150. The new boy had protested and was rewarded with another three days in OP.

The finale was 25 push-ups. Miguel let Hayley, Chelsea, and Cassie do them girl-style, from the knees, but still Cassie's arms shook so hard that she was afraid she would collapse. Collapsing or simply refusing to do something was no refuge. Miguel would just force you back on your feet again.

On her seventeenth push-up, Cassie slipped in the puddle of her own sweat, her still-weak left arm unable to hold her any longer. She landed on her chin on the hard tile. The pain in her jaw was so intense that she thought she had pushed it out of place. She rolled on her back and put her hand to her mouth, feeling her jaw pop as she opened and closed it. Her clothes clung wetly to her.

"You! Start again!" Miguel said. "Twenty push-up."

All this because she had cried on her birthday. With each push-up, Cassie's jaw throbbed and her left arm shook violently. With each dip down, she thought about Rick and how he had betrayed her. And by the time she had completed her push-ups, Cassie had decided that if it were the last thing she did, she would expose Rick and Peaceful Cove to the world. Even if she was forced to wait two years until she was eighteen and legally free to leave, Cassie vowed she would hold this resolve tight inside her, polish it up like a pearl, and finally bring it forth into the light.

part
two

twenty-two

June 1

Cassie was already awake when the screaming began. Even though the Respect Family's room was at the other end of the building from OP, and one floor above, screams penetrated the walls as if they were cardboard. It was impossible to tell if the scream came from a boy or a girl. Cassie had learned that everybody sounded the same when they were being hurt.

When she had first arrived at Peaceful Cove, the screaming had bothered her. Now she found herself wishing that whoever was screaming would just shut up. She wrapped her towel around her head and tried to go back to sleep.

A few minutes later came the wake-up call—Mother Nadine shouting at them to get up. She was always grouchy in the mornings. In silence they got up, bunched up their sheets, and folded their wooden beds against the wall. The room was now completely bare, except for the row of battered milk crates at one end.

Cassie found the crate labeled with her last name. In went her sheet and her pajamas. As quickly as possible, Cassie put on her underwear and the least soiled of her uniforms. She had been here six weeks now, but even if it had been six years she didn't think she could get used to the complete lack of privacy.

Mother Nadine was leaning against the wall with her eyes

closed, so Cassie risked a smile at Hayley as she stood on tiptoes to stack her crate. Cassie was rewarded with a wink. From watching Hayley, Cassie had learned how much she could get away with. And it was quite a bit. Most of the staff didn't have the energy or the will to ride the kids all the time. They took catnaps, read magazines, flirted with each other or sometimes the older kids. Only the sadistic ones—and they were a minority—tried to find ways and reasons to hurt them.

Clutching their toothbrushes and towels, the Respect Family lined up single file and went out into the hall, becoming part of the silent commotion. In family groups of twenty, two hundred young men and women spilled downstairs and into the first-floor hallway. Even in flip-flops, their feet made enough noise that a few people risked a whisper or two of conversation.

Out in the courtyard, they lined up for head count. The day was already hot, the sky a hard blue bowl turned over them. The only sound, aside from the crash of the waves, was the guards counting in Spanish. Across the yard, the boys had lined up in their family groups. Occasionally, people would rub the sleep from their eyes or yawn, but for the most part they were still, hands dangling at their sides, staring at some invisible point in front of them.

As she did every morning, Cassie looked at the sea out of the corner of her eye. The ocean, with its infinite stretch of horizon, was like a taste of freedom. As she watched the white-capped waves roll in, Cassie wondered if it were true that every seventh wave was higher than the ones before.

She had only gotten to the fourth wave when the guards finished counting, then shouted the totals into their walkie-talkies. Since it was Wednesday, one of the days that their family showered, Tania, the guard working with the Respect Family, jerked her head in the direction of the showers.

A single pipe ran over the twenty wooden stalls, spilling water out of twenty separate holes. Like the rest of the girls, Cassie hung her uniform on a hook, then stood with her arms crossed tight across her breasts. *"Ándale,"* Tania said, and she turned the handle that ran water through the pipe. There was a collective gasp as cold water poured onto their heads.

They had three minutes. Quickly and mechanically, Cassie showered, using the small blue sliver of soap that dozens of other kids had used before her. After shaking two ants off her toothbrush, she brushed her teeth. The water went off, and Cassie dried herself.

As she dressed again, she saw a scorpion skittering across the wet cement toward her. One of the baby ones, less than an inch across, which meant that it was one of the most dangerous. Until she came here, the only scorpions she had seen had been in paperweights. Cassie quickly slipped on her flip-flops. From the other girls she had learned that you couldn't hesitate. She stepped on it firmly, then scraped the resulting mess off on the edge of the open drain.

Outside the showers Cassie fell back in line, then hung up her towel on the clothesline. She used the pipe by the ditch to rinse the mud from her feet and flip-flops. Some of the girls used this water to brush their teeth. Cassie didn't. She was sure that was why some girls spent so much time on the toilet, crapping their insides out.

After their shower the Respect Family split up to do daily chores. Cassie was in charge of sweeping and mopping their family's room. For the first few weeks Rebecca had watched her, occasionally going so far as to run her fingers over the still-damp tile. Cassie had been the model Level One, not so much for the hope of leaving, but just to go up a level and get some privacy back. Now that she was finally a Level Two, Cassie was left on her own.

Since the room was only about twenty feet square, it didn't take long to finish her mopping. Cassie leaned against the wall and closed her eyes, knowing Mother Nadine's schedule as well as her own. Right about now, their housemother would be out in the courtyard, sharing a cigarette with Father Roberto and trying to flirt in her American-accented Spanish.

When she felt the air change around her, Cassie jumped. But it was only Hayley, who was in charge of cleaning the hallway.

"What's up?" Cassie said, relaxing back against the wall.

"Not much, just chillin'." Hayley closed her eyes. "Just trying to stay out of Mother Nadine's line of sight. Although she isn't as bad as some of the others."

"How many housemothers have you had?"

Hayley started counting on her fingers. "Seven. I heard Mother Nadine got caught having sex with some eleventh-grade boy back when she was teaching in the States, so that's why she's here. It takes a special kind of American to put up with the crap that goes on here. The Mexicans I can understand. They've got to make a living. But Father Gary always likes to have a couple Americans around, so he can trot them out if a parent unexpectedly shows up."

"Parents can come here?"

"It doesn't happen very often—and they're only supposed to come if you're on Level Four and they've gone through a seminar back in the States. But occasionally someone just shows up. That's happened twice since I've been here. Gary has spies at the airport and the border. When he hears somebody's coming, he immediately goes into cover-up mode. The place gets cleaned up, we get real food, and we get to wash our clothes in a machine."

Cassie listened for a long moment to make sure no one was coming, then whispered her obsession. "Hayley, I've got to get out of here."

"It's impossible. I've been here two years, and nobody's made it out. Nobody. Two guys died trying."

Cassie gulped. "How'd they die?"

"They found one in the desert. It's real easy to get turned around out there."

"My watch has this compass ring thingy." Cassie showed it to her, dialing the ring on the outside so that it made a tiny ticking noise. "I don't know how to use it, though," she admitted. "How did the other one die?"

"Tried to jump from the roof, using a broomstick like a pole vault to go over the wall. I've always wondered about that one, though. I heard a noise that night, like a shot."

Cassie put her hand over her mouth. "They wouldn't kill somebody for leaving!"

Hayley shrugged. "Depends on what they were worried someone might say, and who they might say it to. Three years ago, Gary's brother was running another school in Jamaica, but the authorities closed it down because they were putting kids in OP in dog kennels with duct tape across their mouths. You'd think that would give the parents a clue that something was wrong, but no, most of them just arranged for their kids to be shipped here."

"Duct tape and dog kennels? How do you know that?"

"Because I was there."

"Wait. Your mom knew that about the school—about the kennels—and she still let them send you here?"

Hayley shrugged. "She's a pretty high-powered executive. She's hardly ever home. I don't think she knew what to do with a kid after my dad took off. He used to be the, you know, the househusband. Mr. Mom."

"Then why not just put you in a regular boarding school?"

"She didn't think they were strict enough." Hayley's voice was bitter. "She said I was incorrigible. I was smoking, breaking curfew. She would drop me off outside school and I would just cut and hang at the skate—" Suddenly she picked up her broom and began to sweep the already clean floor.

Cassie grabbed for her mop just in time. Mother Nadine appeared in the doorway, hands on hips.

"You don't fool me for one minute, girls." But her protest was halfhearted, and neither Hayley nor Cassie looked up. Things at Peaceful Cove generally went better if you never met anyone's eyes. Finally Mother Nadine barked, "Line up!" They went downstairs, joining the rest of the Respect Family for breakfast.

The meals were laid out on the table—boiled cabbage and fish, one of Cassie's new favorite meals. Back in the States, she had eaten fish only rarely, chicken maybe once every six months, beef and pork never. Now she ate whatever was put in front of her—fat, scraps, organs. Even so, there was never quite enough.

After breakfast, the Respect Family joined the Health Family in one of the classrooms. The morning PGV was about confidence. Cassie had seen it the first week she came, so she only half watched. The tape lasted thirty minutes. The two teacher's aides stood outside in the hall, talking, so instead of taking notes, she wrote a note to Hayley.

"I'm here because I found out my stepdad was prescribing an experimental drug to kids that killed some of them. He was afraid

I was going to tell. But if I don't, more kids will die. I HAVE to get out of here."

Cassie dropped her pencil, then passed her note to Hayley when she bent over to pick it up. Hayley palmed it like a pro. No one was watching, though. Rebecca looked half asleep, her head propped up on her hand. Hayley read the note, then raised her eyebrows and gave one quick nod.

After they had written their two essays and turned them in, it was 9:30. Time for school. Only there was no teaching. Instead, the Mexican chaperones passed out textbooks that more or less corresponded with the grade you would be in if you were in the States. Cassie's dog-eared textbook—*Our American System: An Introduction to Civics*—had been published in 1982. You were expected to teach yourself—to read, take notes, and when you finished a chapter, ask for a multiple-choice test. If you got stuck, you could raise your hand and one of the aides sitting at the back of the room might be able to help.

Cassie finished a chapter on the First Continental Congress and raised her hand. Without making much of an effort, she took the test. The textbook was on her desk, so she could look up any answers she didn't know, but she didn't bother. The first time she had taken a test, she marked down a few answers that she knew, guessed on a bunch more, and turned it in. When she got it back the next day, she had gotten twenty-one out of forty questions right. She had also gotten a B.

From Hayley, Cassie had learned that it was impossible to get anything lower than a B. Peaceful Cove was a five-star boarding school where everyone received a 3.0 average or above.

After lunch and another class, Cassie's family lined up in the hall to do laundry, a weekly chore. They went back upstairs to get their clothes and sheets, then headed outside. Each of them grabbed a white plastic five-gallon bucket and dipped it into the cold ditch water. The guard poured a handful of soap into each bucket. Cassie plunged her clothes in and then rubbed the edges together.

The guard stood in the shadow of the building, smoking a cigarette, his eyes closed. A dozen whispered conversations sprung up. Instead of looking at each other, people kept their eyes on the guard instead, so that conversations had an oddly sideways quality.

When the rest of the girls started whispering about their favorite foods, Hayley leaned closer to Cassie. "Is what you said about your dad true?"

"It's my stepdad, but yeah. He's been testing this new drug, kind of like a super-Prozac for teenagers. It's supposed to do everything Peaceful Cove does to make kids 'better,' only it takes a week or two, not years."

"Some parents would want that." Hayley lifted her uniform from the gray water and began to twist it. "And maybe some wouldn't. Maybe for some, it's just easier not to have their kid around."

"I don't think any parent would want it if they knew that three kids had died taking it. My stepdad found out I planned on telling, and the next thing I knew I was being shipped off here because they supposedly found crystal meth in my room."

"So why do you want to go home so bad? He clearly doesn't want you there."

Cassie thought of Darren. "I have to find someone who will listen before more kids die."

Hayley inched closer. "When I was in Jamaica, I broke out. I waited until the night guard fell asleep and then I broke through the window. But I had no food, no water, no shoes, no money. I was a white girl with red hair running around on the streets of Jamaica. They caught me within two hours. The supervisor told me I would be in OP for three days." Her eyes were flat. "I was in there for a month straight. So if you run, Cassie, you'd better not come back."

twenty-three

June 2

"Hiya! Hiya!" Cassie shouted, waving her arms, running with the other girls toward the goats that had gathered on the field where they played soccer. Twice a week, the Respect Family was allowed outside to play soccer. Really outside—outside the compound walls. Those who had been given consequences stayed behind, assigned to write essays or do worksheets. Just being forced to stay inside was punishment enough. Watching the goats trot away, bleating, ears flicking up and down, Cassie had the uncomfortable feeling that she had probably eaten one of their brothers or sisters the day before.

The Respect and Triumph Families took their positions in the large dirt field littered with rocks. Even though she had only played it a few times before coming to Mexico, Cassie now loved soccer. Outside the walls, she felt free. There were no housemothers, just four guards who did nothing but watch while two families squared off.

Cassie technically played forward, but no one really stayed in their positions. The game started, and in a few seconds it was just a mad scramble for the ball. Like most of the other girls, she played in her bare feet. Cassie might never have learned how to properly kick a soccer ball, but at Peaceful Cove she had become an expert at running people over. All her anger, fear, and frustration found an outlet in scoring points, sprinting up and down the field, and bulldozing anyone who stood in her way.

A hotshot girl from the Triumph Family who used to play on her high school team broke free and started down the field. Cassie managed to dart in front of her. She tried to kick the ball, but instead she kicked the girl. The other girl went down, grabbing her knee. For a second Cassie had the ball to herself and she began to dribble it up the field. Someone grabbed her ponytail, jerked her head back, and threw her to the ground.

PE was the only time of the day it didn't matter what color shorts you wore, it didn't matter that you didn't deserve to be here, it didn't matter if your parents didn't love you, it didn't matter that you might not go home again for years. All that mattered was getting the dusty black-and-white ball into the goal. The girls fought their way through soccer games as if they were fighting for their lives.

Cassie limped off the field. A few minutes later, Hayley joined her, favoring her right knee, although Cassie was pretty sure she was faking.

"I wish there was a way we could take off now, when we're already outside the walls," Cassie whispered to Hayley. She leaned forward to rub the already darkening bruise on her thigh that was the exact same size as another girl's foot.

The guards had a bet riding on this game and were more involved in watching what was happening on the field than what was going on off it.

Hayley shrugged. "You know how fast they would be on us? We'd be a year's salary apiece running around in flip-flops. We wouldn't get more than a hundred yards." She turned to look at the guards, then slipped a piece of paper folded impossibly small from her bra. "Still want to know how to use that compass ring on your watch?" She pressed it into Cassie's hand.

Without unfolding it or even looking at it, Cassie tucked it into her own bra. "Where did you get it?"

Hayley's grin was proud. "You know that new nurse, the one who looks up stuff on the Internet all the time because she never really graduated from nursing school? I told her I was feeling weak and dizzy, and she let me lie down for a while. As soon as she went to the bathroom, I got on the Timex website. I had the instructions printed out before she got back."

"You shouldn't have taken that chance! She could have sent you to OP for weeks!"

Hayley shrugged, feigning nonchalance. "Just promise me that you'll tell everyone about this place when you leave."

"When I leave?" Panic surged through Cassie. "But you said you would go with me. I need you!"

Hayley wouldn't meet her eyes. "Two people will be twice as easy to find."

"But the way I figure it, you need two people to get home! Two people to make sure we're going the right direction, to help each other climb up those hills, to take turns so one can watch while the other sleeps." Cassie felt desperate. She wouldn't—maybe even couldn't—do it alone. "It's like swimming. You know how they say you should never swim without a buddy?"

Hayley still didn't answer.

Cassie put her hand on Hayley's freckled arm. "Please say you'll do it with me. I'm too scared to do it on my own."

Hayley heaved a sigh. "Look, I'm bad luck. And I would just slow you down. Look how fast you can run across that field. I get twenty feet and I'm panting. All that smoking probably screwed up my lungs." Her gaze finally connected with Cassie's pleading eyes. "Come on, I got you the directions for the watch, didn't I?"

Cassie gave a short shake of her head. "Please. I can't do it without you. I need you. Please?" She hadn't meant to, but her voice broke in the middle of the word.

After what seemed an eternity, Hayley nodded. "All right. I'll come with you. But you'll have to figure out how. I've thought about it and thought about it, and I can't see any way of getting out."

twenty-four

June 3

When the Respect Family filed into the courtyard on their way to head count the next afternoon, they saw two men holding a tall blond girl between them. Cassie flinched. It was Marty and JJ. The two men looked at her without recognition, just one of three dozen girls all dressed the same. The girl they held looked otherworldly to Cassie. Her clothes were so clean! She wore a pink T-shirt, cutoff shorts, two string anklets, and white, silver-striped Adidas. Her shirt stopped short of her belly and announced "How Hot Am I?" Even though you could tell by her face that she was exhausted, she had the most erect posture Cassie had ever seen.

Tears had left shiny tracks down the girl's face. As Cassie thought about what the girl would have to undergo next, she felt her stomach clench.

After dinner, they headed back up to their room for a feedback meeting. The girls from the Respect Family sat in a circle on the floor, legs tucked to one side, while Hector stood outside the open door, laboriously writing up his shift-change report. For a few minutes it was possible to hold hushed conversations before Mother Nadine came into the room. Then they would have the "opportunity" to stand up and "share," or offer "feedback."

Hayley had started to whisper something to Cassie when the

guard stalked into the room. "Who is talking?" Hector asked in heavily accented English. "Who?"

They sat silently, as still as trapped animals. His eyes scanned the room, moving slowly from face to face, searching for a hint of guilt. Everyone suddenly became interested with things on the floor or the backs of their hands, avoiding all eye contact. He only left when Mother Nadine came in.

Cassie hated feedback nearly as much as OP. OP was about your body; feedback was about your mind.

Stephanie was the first to her feet. She had been at Peaceful Cove for over a year. She would have been vaguely pretty—with blond hair, blue eyes, and a heart-shaped face—if she hadn't had angry red zits all over her cheeks and nose. She moved as if she wished she were invisible—head down, shoulders curled over. As a Level Four, she was allowed to look people in the eyes, but she acted as if she were still a Level One.

"I'm really scared." Her voice was high-pitched and babyish. "I'm scared I'm getting anorexia again. It's not so much not eating—even if it's easy not to eat much here—it's more just the way it feels. I hate myself. I feel so disgusting." She made a fist and hit herself, hard, on the thigh. Cassie, who was sitting next to her, could see the red mark her fist had left. "I feel so insecure. I didn't think it was going to come back. And now I don't know what to do. My parents had to hospitalize me in seventh grade because I only weighed seventy-five pounds. I felt the same way then as I do now, like I'm always going to be alone. I try to pretend that everything is okay—but I know that's how I'm going to end up." Tears were running down her face, and she gulped air, the words almost random. "Like, if I get a Cat. Two, I feel like I'm letting everyone down."

Cassie wanted nothing more than to give Stephanie a hug, to

say "shush" over and over until she quieted. The way Cassie's mom used to do. Her mom would hold her until Cassie was able to find a quiet place inside herself, and build from that. But that wasn't how feedback worked.

Finally, Stephanie sat down. Hands went up for feedback. Mother Nadine, who had been looking out the window, turned and pointed at Rebecca.

Rebecca glared at Stephanie. "No one else is thinking about you. Why do you think anyone notices you?"

Mother Nadine nodded and pointed at another girl, Jamie.

"Don't you get it? The purpose of being here, and getting consequences, is to teach you how to pick yourself up. If you don't mess up, you go home." Jamie sounded bored, like a waitress rattling off the lunch specials. It was clear that she'd said this a million times.

"Have you ever thought that maybe you *are* too fat?" This from Samantha, whose two years at Peaceful Cove had whittled her down to about a size zero. But Stephanie was even skinnier, too thin, in Cassie's opinion.

Cassie couldn't stand it anymore. Even though Mother Nadine hadn't pointed at her, she said, "You're not too fat. You're just sad at having to be here. And since being here is out of your control, you control the one thing you can—how much you eat."

Mother Nadine pointed at Cassie. "Sit down. I didn't call on you for feedback. That's a Cat. One offense. You'll have to do ten— no, fifteen—worksheets tomorrow during PE. And Stephanie will have to do them, too. Because Jamie's right, Stephanie. The only way things will work for you *is* to work the program."

Mother Nadine turned her attention back to Cassie. It was clearly her turn to get picked on. "Right, Cassie, I want to hear something private, right now. Or do you want to go to OP?"

As fast as she could, Cassie went through an inventory in her head. What would hurt the least to say? She had already learned that if you told real secrets, they would be used against you later. Last week a girl had said she was afraid her boyfriend wouldn't wait for her, and a few days later Mother Nadine had her up in front of the group and was saying, "You don't think he's waiting, do you? He's laughing at you behind your back. How many of your friends do you think he's sleeping with right now?"

"I think my butt's too big," Cassie started.

Mother Nadine cut her off. "I'm not listening to that. That's not deep. You've got to work the program, only you're not." She opened the door into the hall and leaned out. "Guard! I need a guard to take someone to OP." She gave Cassie a smile over her shoulder. And the smile said that Cassie had until the guard got in the room to give Mother Nadine something better.

Like a rat trapped in a maze, Cassie frantically tried to think of a way out. Every idea seemed a dead end. Hector appeared in the doorway. "My stepfather looks at me too long if he sees me coming out of the bathroom after a shower," she blurted out. It was a lie, but one that she could not get in trouble over.

There was a long silence while Mother Nadine digested this. Finally, she said, "It's all right, Hector," and he went away.

Cassie's feeling of relief was short-lived. Mother Nadine turned back to her with a smile.

"So, what are you wearing when you come out of the bathroom?"

"A towel." Mother Nadine raised an eyebrow. Cassie went on. "It's a big towel and it's my personal bathroom—it's right next door to my room."

"So are you trying to cause trouble? Do you think you're like some cliché out of a bad movie, the teenage girl running around in nothing but a towel? You do that just because you *want* him to look at you, isn't that right?"

"No, I don't," Cassie said, stung. "I try not to take a shower when he's even around, but sometimes he just is."

"You think you're like that girl Lolita," Heather said.

Rebecca chimed in, "You've got a really bad attitude—and you don't have the body you think you do."

"Listen up, girls!" Mother Nadine clapped her hands. "There's an important lesson here. If you dress and act provocatively, if you put yourself at risk—then you get taken advantage of. No always means no—but you've got to look at how you market yourself."

Everyone nodded in agreement. And so it went, the girls all piling on, until somehow, mysteriously, Mother Nadine judged it had been enough and went on to the next poor victim.

Dinner was a bun and cheese, one of Cassie's favorite meals. She nibbled on it slowly, saving every bite, while she listened to the last audiotape: *Lessons in Obtaining Serenity Through Effective Problem Solving.* The dinner tape was always the longest and hardest to listen to. It went on forever, repeating its stilted and ungrammatical lessons. Cassie was tired and she just wanted to finish eating and go to bed.

Finally, the tape was over and they walked single file back into the classrooms for reflections. There, they wrote down what they had memorized from the tapes they had heard and watched that day and turned the papers in to the guard. He would give them to Martha in the morning. She would review Cassie's work and write down in her book, "Student is making significant progress."

During reflections you could also write to your parents. You could even write the truth, if you wanted. But because your parents had already been given the parent handbook and warned that you would lie, it was hard to think of what to write.

Tonight, Cassie tried again to think of a way to let her mom know how bad it really was. Something that would cause her to realize the truth, something that would touch her mom so deeply that she wouldn't turn to Rick, but would instead get on a plane and fly down to get Cassie.

"I really miss you, Mom. I'm sorry if I haven't been the daughter you wanted me to be. I hope I can be home in time to help with the baby." It wasn't enough, she knew, but it was the best she could do. Maybe her mom would think about pulling her out to help with her new brother.

"Oh, I almost forgot, Cassie," Mother Nadine said. "You got a letter." As a Level Two, Cassie was allowed to get letters, as long as they passed Martha's scrutiny. It was rumored that she kept at least seventy-five percent.

Dear Cassie—

I miss you so much! The house seems so quiet without you here. The doctor has put me on bed rest. I won't be able to live a normal life until I'm 38 weeks pregnant, at which point the baby is officially ready. It's like I'm a supermarket turkey and everyone is waiting for one of those little red thermometer things to pop out to show that I'm done. I'm only allowed to get up to go to the bathroom, can you believe that? Other than that, I have to be lying down, although I can prop my head and shoulders up. I read, watch TV, or use Rick's laptop, but time just crawls. I'm going to ask Rick to see if he can talk them into making an exception and letting me call you when the baby is born.

I really miss you. Remember back in our old house how we would stay up late on Friday watching movies and eating popcorn and ice cream? Those were some good times, weren't

*they? I hope you can be home soon. Rick says it shouldn't be
much longer until you are ready. Maybe you'll be home
by Christmas.*

*I'm going to put this in the envelope before Rick comes
home, but I'm sure he would send his love, as I do.*

Love,
Mom

Cassie couldn't breathe. Her tears were stuck inside her, and
she refused to let them out. Not in front of Mother Nadine. It felt
like she had swallowed something sharp that was now lodged
below her collarbone. How long would Rick keep lying to her
mom? And how long would her mom keep believing him? After
Christmas he would probably tell her that the Stateside rep said
Cassie might be home for her birthday. And then her birthday
would come and go and he would make up another excuse. And by
that time, her mom would be busy with the new baby. It might be
years before Jackie saw through his lies.

It was clear that the only person who was going to get Cassie
out of Peaceful Cove was Cassie.

twenty-five

June 4

The next day, they stood in the courtyard, waiting for the guards to finish their evening head count. Mother Nadine stood next to Cassie, rooting in her purse, looking for her cigarettes. Sometimes Cassie thought she delighted in smoking in front of the girls, often only minutes after they had listened to a taped lecture about how smoking would turn their lungs black.

With the purse pouched open, Cassie saw something amid the jumble of pens and tampons and makeup. Something as small as a calculator. But it was a cell phone.

A phone! She quickly looked away, so that Mother Nadine wouldn't catch her staring and read her mind. If she had a phone, Cassie could call her dad and he would come for her. She knew he would.

Their relationship had always been weighed down by his guilt at leaving, his guilt at starting a new family. When she was thirteen, he had missed her birthday, hadn't even called her until three days later, when his new wife was visiting her sister with his new kids. He sounded like he was drunk. He also sounded like he was crying.

But no matter what he said or did, Cassie always knew her dad would be there for her if she really needed him. She didn't know where Jackie had told him Cassie had gone, but she was sure it was a lie. And she was also sure that if she could just talk to her dad for five minutes, he would be on the next plane down.

The first problem would be to get her hands on the phone. Mother Nadine was never too far from her purse. But Cassie and Hayley were a team. If one of them could create a distraction, the other could get the phone.

The next morning Cassie snatched a moment to talk as they hung up their towels after showering. To Cassie's surprise, Hayley balked.

"But how do you know he'll come?"

"He's my dad."

Hidden by the line of towels, Hayley snorted and shrugged. "So?"

"*So!* He's my dad. Of course he'll come for me once he realizes what's going on here."

"You think he doesn't already know? You think the parents don't know what's going on? Of course they do. It's just more convenient for them if they pretend that Peaceful Cove is just as good as they say in their brochures."

"Girls!" the guard, Tania, barked. She blew her whistle before Cassie could ask if Hayley would still help her even if she didn't believe it would work. Even if she thought it was a lost cause.

But Cassie should have known. Two days later during reflections, when everyone was exhausted and looking forward to bed, Hayley began waving her hand over her head.

"What is it, Hayley?" Mother Nadine's voice held a note of surprise. Hayley wasn't the kind of girl to ask for help or permission.

"Can you come look at my letter to my mom, tell me if you think it's okay?"

As Mother Nadine got to her feet, Hayley shot Cassie a look.

The brown purse was on the floor, right next to Cassie's thigh. And unzipped. As Mother Nadine stood up, and while everyone was still looking at Hayley, marveling at her request, Cassie mimed a yawn. She stretched and let her hand drop into the purse. Like a miracle, she felt her fingers close around the slim plastic case. She leaned forward, faking a stretch, and tucked the phone into the top of her panties, underneath her shorts. Cassie just prayed the elastic would hold.

Now she had to find a way to make a call. And soon, before Mother Nadine noticed her phone was gone. In the best possible scenario, Cassie would be able to make the call and return the phone before its absence was discovered.

She had planned on calling from the bathroom, since it was the only time she could count on being alone. But now she thought about how much the small room echoed. And the door didn't lock. And Hector was working tonight. He was always looking for an excuse to open the door and catch sight of a girl peeing.

Mother Nadine was still leaning over Hayley, happily engaged in a lecture about all the things Hayley had done wrong. Before she could think better of it, Cassie bent forward and thrust her fingers down her throat. Dinner that night had been rancid-tasting pork. Her stomach had been sour ever since. Vomit poured out of her mouth almost instantly, splattering her legs and feet and the floor. The other girls around her squealed and scattered.

"You're going to have to clean that up yourself, Cassie," Mother Nadine rapped out. "Go down to the laundry and get some rags." Cassie was already on her feet when she added, "And take Rebecca with you."

Cassie should have realized that there was no way Mother Nadine would let her go anyplace by herself. Still, there was no turning back.

It was strange and more than a little eerie to walk down the empty, darkened corridors, taking care to skirt around the buckets that had been set out to catch the drips from the leaking roof. Two hundred people lived here, but all you saw was a spill of light from under each family's closed door. No sound, aside from a few murmurs.

The laundry room was next to the kitchen. Most of the cupboard doors were locked, but one stood ajar, the lock dangling. Rebecca went to close it. For a moment she stood mesmerized by the sight of a cardboard box filled with the little cracker-and-cheese packets that were sometimes doled out to upper-level students.

"I love these things," she said slowly. Moving as slowly as a sleepwalker, she picked up one of the packets.

"Maybe I'll just go along and get those rags," Cassie said, feeling the lump of the phone pressing against her stomach.

"Okay," Rebecca said absently. Cassie scurried into the laundry room, pulled out the phone, and turned it on. Since she was in Mexico, did she have to dial a series of numbers to reach the United States? Cassie didn't know, and she didn't know what those numbers would be, anyway. She had gathered that Peaceful Cove wasn't that far from the border, though, and how would the cell phone know where it was? She pressed the number 1, then the 503 area code, then her dad's home number.

After five rings, a man's voice, sounding distracted, said, "Hello?"

At the sound of his voice, Cassie's throat choked with tears.

"Daddy," she managed to gasp out, but she couldn't make anything else squeeze past.

His tone sharpened. "Cassie? Cassie—is that you? Where are you? Are you home?"

She swallowed hard, forcing down her tears, forcing herself to speak softly when she wanted to scream. "I'm in Mexico. Daddy, Daddy, please come get me. It's called Peaceful Cove." Her words were running into each other, but she couldn't make herself slow down. The connection crackled and her own words echoed back to her through the earpiece.

"But honey, I don't have formal custody over you. I can't do anything if your mom decides to send you to a different school."

"A school!" Unconsciously, she had raised her voice. It echoed in the small room. She quickly lowered it again. "Daddy, it's a prison here. They beat us."

"Beat you—do you mean somebody hits you? Your mom and I may have our differences, but she would never send you anyplace like that."

"But it *is* like that, Daddy. There's kids here with missing teeth. If you love me, please believe me. You have to help. They hurt us every day. Why do you think it's in Mexico? There aren't any rules here—"

Cassie's ponytail was yanked back so hard that her teeth closed on her tongue. The phone fell from her hand. Rebecca snatched it up and pressed the off button.

"What are you doing?" She began to scream and slap Cassie with open hands, a flurry of blows that landed on her head, neck, breasts. "I have to get out of here, do you hear me? I have to get out of here! You stupid little bitch! Do you know how much trouble I could get into? I can't go back to being a Level One! I can't!" Her hands were closed now, fists raining down. Cassie backed up against the dryer. She stumbled and fell to her knees, then curled into a ball, her hands cupping the back of her neck, bent arms shielding her head. Being down on the floor was worse. Rebecca was kicking her now, and her legs were stronger than her arms.

Her foot connected with Cassie's cheek, and Cassie felt teeth move in her jaw.

Then suddenly, everything stopped.

Cassie rolled her eyes up, trying to see what was happening without exposing any more of her face.

It was Father Gary, his face cherry red. He was shaking Rebecca like a rag doll. "Who did she call?"

"Her dad," Rebecca mumbled sullenly.

"Are you twice as much a fool! If one of her family flies here and sees her covered with bruises, then what do you think will happen? I don't need another parent going to the State Department. Take her to OP, but you tell the guards there is not going to be a mark on her. I don't want to see as much as a rash. I'll start doing damage control."

twenty-six

June 7

"What is Peaceful Cove about, people? It's about learning self-discipline and respect. Learning to be respectful of ourselves, respectful of others, respectful of the gifts we have so generously been given. And yet what do I see when I look around? I see cobwebs, I see weeds, I see dirt and disorder."

The rows of teens stood silent in the courtyard, heads bowed, unmoving, as Father Gary paced back and forth in front of him. He had to raise his voice to be heard over the drumming raindrops that hit the hard-packed earth and bounced back up again. His white shirt was soaked through, revealing the outline of his belly, the hairs on his chest. His face was red, his gestures quick and abrupt.

"You have allowed this beautiful spot to mirror your own interior disorder. Any visitor would immediately jump to the wrong conclusions about the hard and worthy work we are doing here. So for the next few days we will be working to make our external world harmonious with what we are learning inside ourselves. This is for our own benefit, as much as it might be for any visitors. But if we do end up having visitors, and if any one of you finds occasion to lie to them—well, know this, your lies will be rewarded with weeks in OP. If not months."

They were lined up as if for head count, but instead of the guards yelling into their walkie-talkies, they had Father Gary warning that they were now in what he termed a "Code Red situation." The regular schedule was suspended so that they could make Peaceful Cove resemble, in even a passing way, the image presented in the brochure, before Cassie's father turned up. If he turned up.

For the next thirty-six hours, Peaceful Cove was cleaned from top to bottom. Students were sent up on the roofs with buckets of tar to plug the holes, or handed cans of insecticide until the whole building reeked of some Mexican brand of Raid. Clothes were washed in what was normally the staff's washing machine. Even the food improved—there was meat at every meal, and it was more or less identifiable.

Even though everyone's life had improved for the moment, the other girls treated Cassie like a pariah. No one whispered to her or even met her eye in an unobserved moment. The only one who still treated her the same was Hayley. They had both been busted back down to Level One.

The second day after she had called her father, Cassie and a half dozen Respect Family members were working in the laundry. It was hot and so humid, it felt like she was working in a steam room. She couldn't even make a face at Hayley, who had been summoned by Hector after lunch, although Hayley hadn't been doing anything wrong that Cassie could see.

What would she do if her dad didn't come? Or if he came but didn't believe her? It didn't pay to get on the wrong side of Father Gary, and now Cassie was so far on the wrong side, she couldn't even see daylight. Her dad *had* to come, and she had to persuade him to take her home.

Lost in thought, Cassie leaned down to get another basket of grimy sheets. Next to it was a pair of men's shoes. Her heart leapt. Father Gary. His footsteps had been muffled by the thumping of the dryers. He was looking down at her, his eyes narrowed.

"Come with me. We need to have a talk."

Cassie followed him past kids sweeping the yard, scrubbing grime from the windows, and whitewashing the concrete walls. Father Gary took Cassie into the small room where she had had her first introduction to Peaceful Cove.

Father Gary looked calm, and that scared Cassie more than if he had been angry. Now he leaned back in his chair, stroking his beard, his eyes hooded. "You like Hayley, don't you?" It wasn't really a question, but she nodded anyway. "I've just had word that your biological father has driven across the border. He'll be here in half an hour. That's why Hayley's gone. She's with Hector now, off the grounds." He took a walkie-talkie from his belt and pressed the button on the side. "Hector. Come in, Hector."

There was an answering crackle of static. *"¿Sí?"*

"Have Hayley say *hola* to Cassie."

"Hi, Cassie." If she hadn't seen Hayley being marched away by Hector, Cassie wouldn't have known her voice. It was all wrong, too high-pitched, and strangled-sounding. Had he hurt her?

"*Gracias.* That's all, Hector, over and out." Father Gary switched off the walkie-talkie and regarded her calmly. "We run a good program here, Cassie, a good program. We change lives every day. Kids who have graduated from Peaceful Cove have gone to college, gone on to good jobs, gone on to be good mothers and fathers. They leave here having learned self-discipline and self-respect." He leaned forward. "I will not have you jeopardize this program. I will not have you put yourself above the good of one hundred and eighty other students. Do you understand me?"

Cassie nodded. She realized that Father Gary believed his own words, and for some reason that frightened her even more. His eyes drilled into her until she opened her mouth and said, "Yes, I understand."

"Good. Now if, while your father is here, you say or do anything that puts this program at risk, then I turn on the walkie-talkie. I don't even need to say anything. Hector will just hear the crackle and know that he can do anything he wants to your friend. Anything. You don't want that, do you?"

Cassie took a deep shuddering breath, but she couldn't delay the inevitable. Finally, she said, "No. No, sir."

Father Gary smiled. "Good. I don't mean to make this difficult for you, Cassie. You're like a high-spirited horse that won't be broken to the saddle. But there comes a time when we all must accept our burdens."

twenty-seven
June 8

When Cassie first saw her father, she thought she was going to faint. She swayed on her feet, and Father Gary put his arm around her to steady her, his grip like iron.

Her dad ran across the beaten earth of the courtyard toward her and she stumbled toward him. Then his arms were tight around her shoulders, holding her so close that she couldn't take a breath. She wanted to whisper in his ear, warn him somehow that they were being watched, that she would have to lie. But how could she, without risking that her father wouldn't understand, wouldn't question her aloud? Father Gary was only ten feet away.

Finally, they pulled apart. Her father looked tired, with dark circles under his eyes. Cassie couldn't believe he was really here, in a dress shirt, loosened tie, and pressed pants, looking as alien as if Santa Claus had suddenly appeared in the flesh.

"They tried to tell me I couldn't visit you until you reached the upper levels, but I said, screw that, my daughter sounds desperate." He looked her up and down, his hands still on her shoulders. "But Cassie, you're so—so tan. And thin. You look great!"

Great!?! Did her dad think Peaceful Cove was some kind of fat camp where Cassie had been trimmed down and tanned to perfection?

"It's just a farmer tan," she said, pulling up her sleeve so that he could see her white upper arm. "It's not like we're lying on the beach or anything."

Father Gary frowned at her, but she didn't think she had said anything that could get her in trouble. Or, more important, get Hayley in trouble.

"I guess you couldn't even get to the beach, could you?" her dad asked, looking past her at the hundred-foot drop to the endless line of waves.

"Oh, the children on the upper levels go on outings," Father Gary interjected smoothly. "The beach, horseback riding, shopping at the local farmer's market. But they have to earn their privileges."

With difficulty, Cassie kept her face neutral. Father Gary put out his hand, and Cassie's dad shook it automatically. "Gary Fisk, Peaceful Cove's director. And you must be Cassie's dad, Mr. . . . ."

"It's Steve. Steve Streng. When Cassie phoned me, she said kids were being beaten here."

Father Gary's laugh sounded unforced. "Has your ex-wife shared our handbook with you? We warn parents about this behavior right up front. Making up stories—lying, if you will—is one of the typical stages teens go through before they settle down to the hard work of change. There's always a time period where they will do or say anything rather than admit they need to change." He waved his arm expansively. "You are free to move around the grounds and talk to any of the kids you want. I won't deny we run a tight ship. This is a tough program where inappropriate attitudes and choices are confronted and redirected. It's not comfortable here. It's not *meant* to be comfortable. Peaceful Cove has been specially designed to motivate young people to do the hard work they need to so that they can leave here and go home to be with their families."

"Still, I want to talk to my daughter. Now. Alone."

Cassie's heart leapt. Her dad wasn't buying any of this.

"Certainly," Father Gary said smoothly. "When you're done talking, I'll give you the fifty-cent tour." He led them inside and into a small room that held two chairs. The OP room, only for once it was empty. And it was clean. All the stains had been scrubbed from the tile. Over her dad's shoulder, Father Gary gave Cassie a look. It was clear his choice of rooms was deliberate. Every minute would remind her of Hayley. Father Gary left the room, but he didn't close the door completely. Cassie listened for the sound of his footsteps, uncertain just how far away he had gone.

"How are you, honey? Really. I want you to tell me the truth."

"Oh, Daddy," Cassie managed to choke out, before the words and the emotions all got stuck in her throat.

He hugged her to him and she let herself relax into his shoulder. For a second, she felt safe. But only for a second.

"You said they beat you." He ran his hands up and down her arms, stepped back to look at her legs. "I don't see any marks."

She still had scratches on her breasts and bruises on her back from Rebecca's attack. But then she thought of Hayley. She choked out the necessary lie. "Maybe what I should have said is that they're really strict."

"Strict! Jesus, Cassie, what do you expect after the crap you pulled? After you called me, I talked to your mom. And she explained everything. You're only in tenth grade! I mean, drugs? How could you? I know it's been hard the last couple of years, moving and all, maybe me and Ruby having kids, but . . ." His voice trailed off. His brown eyes reminded her of a dog's, faithful and disappointed.

She opened her mouth, and closed it again. She was in dangerous territory now. And then it came to her.

"Dad, since I've been here, I've been thinking about when I was little. Remember when we watched those Disney videos together?" *Pinocchio,* she willed him to say. And then he might start thinking about what was true and what was lies. "That video we watched over and over?"

His gaze softened. "You mean *Dumbo?* Is that what the problem was? Were you just feeling too much the odd girl out at your new school?"

She tried again. "I wasn't thinking of that movie, Dad, but the other one. The one with the"—she lowered her voice—"the cricket? Remember that one?"

He shook his head, and it was clear he wasn't getting it. His eyes shone with unshed tears.

Cassie reached out and squeezed his hand. "Daddy, I'm really sorry, okay?"

He looked at her for a long time, really looked in a way he hadn't for years, maybe not forever. "You're sorry."

"Yes."

"Can you promise me that you would never use drugs again?"

This was easy. "Yes."

He looked at her, then pinched the bridge of his nose. "I said the same thing when your grandpa caught me smoking pot. I lied about it. But I was in college. And it was only pot. But now—now your life could be on the line, Cassie."

"But, Dad," she started, and then stopped. She didn't know what else to do.

"Come on," he said, taking her arm. "Let's go take the tour. I want to see for myself what this place is like."

They found Father Gary in his office. Was it her imagination, or did he look smug, as if he had heard everything they had said? He pushed back his chair and stood up. "Ready for that tour now?"

Following Father Gary, they walked into the two classrooms where American teachers were actually teaching. Barely hearing Father Gary's smooth patter, Cassie swung from panic to fear and back again as she weighed spending two more years here against Hayley being beaten, raped, or worse.

"She sleeps on a board?" Cassie's dad asked incredulously when he looked into the Respect Family's room. If only he could see her bed the way it regularly was. Today, all the towels had been camouflaged by new white pillowcases, and the beds had been left folded down from the wall.

"That's all part of the program. The accommodations are deliberately simple and basic, not nearly as nice as your home. We make them want to go back home because they've learned to appreciate it."

"I don't know," Cassie's father said slowly. "It doesn't look as bad as I thought it would, but it still seems pretty austere. Maybe I should just take you back home, Cassie. I mean, you couldn't live with us, we just don't have the room, but maybe if you went to counseling. I mean, if you promised to behave . . ."

Startling them both, Father Gary barked out, "Do you want her to die?"

"Of course not!" Her dad took a step back, looking offended and skeptical.

"All the counseling in the world will never change someone's heart if they aren't ready to change. This is a shock point to force Cassie out of her comfort zone, to make her see what her choices have done to her and to you. Do you know what happens to kids who get removed from the program prematurely, before they've even started to progress?" He emphasized each of his next words. "They get *worse*. They use more drugs, drink more alcohol, have more unprotected sex. The only difference is that now they've caught on that their parents are watching, so they make sure they cover their tracks. Do you really want to be responsible for that?"

Father Gary stared at her dad hard before continuing. "I have watched literally hundreds of kids come and go from Peaceful Cove. Some left when they were ready to, others before it was time. And I've heard the stories of what happened to those who left too soon. Some of them ended up dropping out of school and working at McDonald's, some on the street, some selling their bodies. And some of them ended up dead. Do you want to risk that?"

"I—I just don't know. I love my daughter and want to do what's right. And I don't know if this place is the right place for her." Her dad's shoulders sagged. Now he sounded uncertain. He looked at Cassie. "Maybe I should talk to your mother about putting you in a Stateside school. Someplace where we could visit you. It's not good to cut you off from everyone."

As Cassie's dad was speaking, Father Gary picked up the walkie-talkie from his desk, began to run his fingers up and down the side, not quite touching the transmit button. He didn't even look at Cassie. He didn't have to. The message was loud and clear.

Cassie summoned the words to her lips, even managed something of a smile. "After listening to you, Dad, I realize that maybe it's not so bad here. I'm learning a lot." She looked over at Father Gary. "A whole lot." He nodded once, but her father didn't notice.

"Are you sure? You sounded so upset on the phone."

"I was lonely when I called." She suddenly had an idea. "Since then I've made friends here. There's this one girl, Hayley—"

"Can I meet her?"

"Sorry," Father Gary said smoothly, before Cassie could say anything else. "She's on one of those outings I talked about." He looked at Cassie. His finger was poised over the button.

Cassie realized there was nothing else she could do, not unless she was willing to sacrifice Hayley. "I've had the last two days to think, Dad. I think it would be best if I stayed here."

He looked at her closely. Part of her wanted to cry when she saw the expression in his eyes. Doubt mingled with relief. "Are you sure?"

"I'm sure." Cassie gave him another hug, swift and hard. How many years would it be before she touched him again?

twenty-eight

In the days after Cassie's dad left, Cassie and Hayley began to plot their escape in earnest. Two hours after Cassie's dad drove away, Hayley had come back from Hector shaking, but had sworn that he hadn't touched her. Still, Hayley seem to have a newfound resolve to leave. Now the only question was how.

On a day when the Respect Family was assigned to yank weeds from the yard, Cassie let her eyes roam over the walls, looking for any rough spots she might use to climb to the top. But the cinder-block wall was new and in good shape. When she stood up to dump her weeds in the trash, she walked as close to the wire mesh fence as she could without attracting the attention of the guards. If you found a way to climb over the fence and past the concertina wire, maybe you could edge along next to it, clinging like a monkey, until you were past the facility. But there was less than a foot of space on the other side of the wire fence before the cliff—often much less. Any slip would be a certain death.

As she walked back, her empty bucket banging against her knee, Cassie's eyes fell on the ditch that ran along the edge of the far wall, just past the laundry lines. The water flowed fast and cool, even in the summer heat. Where it entered the wall and again where it poured into the ocean, the open ditch became a closed metal pipe about three feet across. The water nearly filled the pipe, leaving less than a foot of clearance from the top.

Picking the farthest patch of weeds, Cassie knelt down next to the ditch, eyeing the open mouth of the pipe while her hand slowly reached out for a weed. How long did the pipe stretch underground before it became an open ditch again? She couldn't tell. The pipe was nothing but a black hole. From the times she had played soccer outside the walls, Cassie tried to picture where exactly the pipe ended and the ditch began. She thought about twenty feet of it were buried. Maybe thirty.

Too far to hold your breath, not when you were fighting upstream in a narrow metal tube filled with water. And she was a poor swimmer. When she was five and taking private swimming lessons, Cassie had almost drowned when her teacher went inside to answer the phone. Ever since she had had to fight back panic before she could put her face in the water. Learning to snorkel in Hawaii two years ago had been a triumph, but the water had been warm and buoyant, and thanks to the snorkel she had been able to breathe all she wanted without having to raise her face.

Snorkeling! Maybe that was the answer. She remembered the mesh bag with fins and a mask that her mom had packed. Martha had left the bag in her suitcase. If Cassie could get down to the office and get into the closet again, then the bag should still be inside. And there were so many suitcases, there was bound to be another set for Hayley.

Over the next few days, they began to assemble the pieces they needed for the plan. At night they took turns staying awake until they were sure of the guard's schedule. He rounded once at 11:30, then did not come back again until just before dawn. Using her compass ring and the instructions Hayley had gotten for her, Cassie practiced with her watch until she was sure she knew how to tell where north was. And she and Hayley both kept their eyes open for discarded gum—a "privilege" only open to Level Fours and above. They hid their collection of pieces, pried from the bathroom wall, by wrapping them in Cassie's spare uniform.

"Tonight?" Cassie whispered to Hayley on Thursday evening as they were lined up for head count. She felt light-headed and buzzy.

Hayley gave the slightest of nods. They had checked out the OP room as they walked to head count, and for once it was empty. Mother Nadine had just left for five days of vacation. She had teased them with her upcoming trip to California, where she would enjoy American food, American air-conditioning, and American movies. Some of the Level Sixes had sucked up major before she left, asking Mother Nadine to bring them back news of current fashions and movie stars, asking her to drink a latte for them or eat a bagel. As a substitute housemother, the Respect Family now had Rosa, who normally just passed out textbooks and graded tests when she wasn't gossiping with her friends.

In the bathroom before lights out, Cassie popped the wads of old gum into her mouth. At first it was so dry that it cracked into shards, but then it began to reconstitute itself. Before returning to her family's room, she tucked the lump inside one cheek. As Rosa was leaving, Cassie followed her out in the hall, palming the gum.

"Rosa?"

"¿Si?"

"It's about the math we were studying today. I don't really understand about dividing a polynomial by a monomial." As she spoke, Cassie leaned against the edge of the doorjamb, sheltering it with the small of her back. "Can you explain that to me?" Her fingers poked the gum into the space where the lock would normally click into place. She had practiced the move twice before while cleaning the room, so she knew that the gum would keep the lock from catching.

Mother Nadine would have been suspicious in an instant, but Rosa had a plodding earnestness about her. It was clear from her face that she had no idea what Cassie was talking about. All she said was, "*Mañana*. You go to sleep now."

But of course Cassie didn't sleep. She could feel Hayley watching her even though she never looked over. At 12:30, an hour after the guard's heavy footsteps had echoed down the hall, Cassie began to move as silently as a shadow. Once on her feet, she slowly let the wooden slat that served as her bed fold itself back into place. Across from her, Hayley moved like a mirror image. Cassie saw one pair of eyes flicker open, shining wetly in the darkness, then another. The other girls stayed silent, watching, observing the unspoken code of silence that governed most of the students. It was always safer to pretend that you had seen nothing, knew nothing. At least Rebecca was still truly asleep, one arm flung over her eyes.

Picking her water bottle off the floor, Cassie tiptoed to the door, eased it open, and stepped out into the darkened corridor. Hayley followed. Cassie turned and slowly closed the door, her eyes on the girls in the Respect Family, both those who met her gaze and those who slept on, oblivious. This would be the last time she would see them. She was surprised to find tears pricking her eyes. *I'll tell them what it's like,* she promised them silently as the door closed.

They tiptoed down the hall and then the stairs. Cassie was grateful they were made of cement and couldn't creak to betray their passing. Once on the first floor, where there were no sleeping rooms, she breathed a little easier. Staff, including Father Gary, slept in the short arm of the L, on the third floor.

Hayley glided to the main door, tried the handle, and then turned to give Cassie a thumbs-up. They had been fairly sure—but not certain—that the staff relied on locking kids in their rooms, a cage within the cage of the compound. One worry down.

Now to get supplies. They went around the corner to the main office. Before Hayley turned on the light, Cassie pulled down the blinds. Anyone looking from the other wing of the building might see light leaking around the edges, but that couldn't be helped.

Sliding open Martha's desk drawer, Cassie rooted through pens, paper clips, and candy wrappers. From the jumbled mess, Hayley plucked a red lighter. "Let's take this," she whispered. "Just imagine, tomorrow night we'll be sitting around a campfire. And then maybe by the next morning we'll be in America."

Cassie continued to search through glue sticks and gum wrappers for the keys to the closet. She pushed down a feeling of panic. If they couldn't get inside the closet, her plan wouldn't work.

"What's this?" Hayley said, pulling out a wad of paper-clipped American bills from the very back of the drawer. "Money. Lots of money. I wonder if Gary knows about this. I have a feeling this did not begin life as Martha's money." She split the bills in two and handed one wad to Cassie, motioned for her to tuck it in her bra. "If someone ends up on our heels, try throwing this at them. With any luck they'll get distracted chasing after American money."

Finally, under a bunch of used tissues, Cassie's fingers closed on a set of keys. After a couple of tries, she unlocked the closet. Near the top of the pile, she found her suitcase, with its rainbow ribbon tied around the handle. The first thing she grabbed from the suitcase was the snorkel set in a mesh bag. Then she pawed through the slippery plastic bags her mom had packed until she found the ones with her Nikes and socks. She snatched up clear bags holding a pair of jeans, a baseball cap, and a striped sweater. Stripes! She hadn't seen striped clothes since she entered Peaceful Cove.

Hayley had disappeared into the back of the closet, and now finally emerged with a shocking pink Hello Kitty suitcase. She saw Cassie's expression and shrugged. "What can I say? I was a kid when my mom sent me away."

Going back to the closet, Cassie dug around until she found a backpack. Yanking out empty folders and three-ring notebooks, she imagined a parent carefully packing for a fictitious "campus."

A sound made her head whip around. But it was only Hayley, her fist stuffed in her mouth as she knelt by her open suitcase. She spoke in a strangled whisper. "I don't know what I was thinking. When my mom sent me to Jamaica, I was only twelve. None of this is going to fit me."

"Especially not the shoes, and that's what most important," Cassie said briskly, leaning over her own suitcase again. They didn't have time to lose. "And I don't have another pair that aren't sandals, so start looking. For everything else, you can wear my stuff—we're about the same size. But quick! We've got to get out of here."

She began to open suitcase after suitcase, shoving them aside as quietly as she could when they yielded nothing. Had her mom been the only one who had packed a snorkel set?

"Forget it, Cassie." Hayley had found a pair of Adidas and was busy stuffing them into one of Cassie's plastic bags. "I'll just hold my breath or something."

"It's way too far to do that. When I get to the other side, I'll take off the snorkel and flippers and send them back through the tunnel. If you miss a flipper, it's not the end of the world. You can still pull yourself along with your hands. Just be sure you get the snorkel. I'll send it last so you can be ready."

The office was a mess now, suitcases gaping open, clothes heaped on the floor, stuff piled on Martha's desk. Cassie found another backpack for Hayley and began shoving things in. They each now had shoes, long pants, sweaters, socks, hats, and sunscreen. They had filled their water bottles earlier in the evening. Cassie had even found a single Powerbar in someone's suitcase, although there was no telling how old it was.

Cassie shrugged on her backpack, then pulled out the snorkel from the mesh bag, slipping on the goggles and leaving the mouthpiece dangling. Hayley followed her outside, turning out the light as she left. They slipped down the hall, out the front door, and into the night. Clouds covered the moon.

Even though the air was warm, Cassie started to shake. This was it. They were really doing it. They looked left and right. No guards, no sign of life.

Hayley pulled her pajama top over her head, then found the hole in the fence, wrapped the top in a rock, and pushed it through. They had both managed to keep their bras on when they dressed for bed. Cassie listened for the thunk of it landing, but heard nothing but waves. With any luck, someone would spot it and think they had gone over the fence, buying them some time while they searched the rocks. Without her top, Hayley was all planes and angles, too thin, her bra slack, her white chest and back contrasting strangely with her freckled arms.

They picked their way past the shower shack, ducked underneath the towels, and headed to the ditch. Cassie stepped out of her flip-flops and put one foot into the water. It was colder than she expected. She stepped back. There was no way they could stay, but she was suddenly too frightened to go.

A light went on behind them. They ducked down and turned, shielding their eyes. Someone stood at the front door, sweeping the length of the courtyard with a powerful flashlight. Cassie prayed that they were hidden by the towels.

"Go on without me." Hayley pushed her. "Go! I'll create a distraction."

"What are you talking about?" Cassie hissed. "I'm not leaving you. We'll turn ourselves in."

"No! One of us has to get out and tell people what it's like."

"Then you go!" She tried to thrust the flippers in Hayley's hands.

Hayley's shadowed face suddenly looked old. "My mom doesn't want me. Why do you think she's kept me here? Go on—and tell people about this place. Maybe somebody will pay attention to you."

There was a shout, and Cassie knew they had been spotted.

"I'm not leaving without you!" Cassie grabbed Hayley's arm, but the other girl just spun away from her and began running, grabbing a towel from the line as she went. There was a sudden flare of light. Cassie gasped. Hayley had lit the towel on fire, and now she hollered and twirled it over her head, stamping her feet up and down on the bare earth. In the darkness her blue eyes glowed like silver.

The burning end of the towel flickered, nearly went dark, then brushed against another towel, which suddenly blazed up, orange and red flames throwing that corner of the courtyard into brightness. The flames leapt from towel to towel, racing the length of the clothesline, and then suddenly the thatched roof of the shower stalls was alight. The fire had a sound now, grumbling to itself as it ate. Openmouthed in horror, Cassie looked from the shower stalls to the main building. It was made of stucco—but the roof had been freshly coated with tar. Didn't tar burn?

More shouts in Spanish and English, screams, lights being

switched on. Father Gary appeared in the entrance. The bigger bulk of Martha came up behind him, shouted at him, tugged his free arm. He paid her no mind. His head swiveled from left to right as he scanned the courtyard. Looking for something. Or someone. In the flickering light, Cassie saw that Father Gary held something in his right hand. It wasn't a walkie-talkie or a cell phone. It was a gun.

Cassie snugged the flippers over her feet, put the snorkel mouthpiece between her teeth, and slid into the ditch. The water was so cold that she gasped and nearly lost the mouthpiece.

Cassie had never snorkeled in freshwater before, and she quickly discovered why no one would want to. She wasn't nearly as buoyant as she had been when she and her mom had gone to Hawaii. The heavy pack pushed her down. With her hands, she walked herself forward and into the mouth of the pipe.

It was completely black. When Cassie closed her eyes, it made no difference. Her breathing sped up. She had never been afraid of narrow, constricted spaces before, but then again, she had never been trapped in a narrow pipe filled with water. She pulled herself forward, grabbing frantically for the ridges of the pipe, slick with algae. Her kicks were uncoordinated, her legs moving in a frenzy, desperate to propel her through and out of the pipe.

She was no longer thinking about Peaceful Cove. Her world had narrowed to the size of a three-foot-wide metal tube filled with water. The pipe wasn't even wide enough to swing her arms overhead, so she was half swimming, half crawling. Every few feet, her hips and knees bumped painfully against the bottom. Her mouth ached from biting down on the plastic mouthpiece. What if the water got deeper or the pipe narrowed down?

Suddenly, water was in her mouth, finding its way down the snorkel despite the float valve. She had to stand up, she had to.

Cassie thrashed, wanting nothing more than to feel air on her face. But the pipe was too small to kneel in.

Something heavy and soft smacked her on top of the head. When she tried to push it away, her fingers sank into squishy fur. Some kind of animal, dead and rotting in the water. A wave of nausea rolled through her as she clawed it away. The pipe was never going to end. She was going to die in this pipe, die like this animal had.

And then suddenly she felt the space change around her. There was cold air on her back. She was out in the open ditch in the field beyond the compound.

Coughing, Cassie crawled out of the ditch. She opened her waterlogged backpack, shoved on her shoes, and began to run.

twenty-nine

June 17

Stumbling over rocks, trying to avoid the spiky bushes, Cassie kept on, shaking as much from fear as from cold. The only way out was forward. To keep moving and to get as far as possible before they took a head count and figured out who was missing. Before they forced Hayley to tell what she knew.

She turned around to look at Peaceful Cove. A dark column of smoke blotted out the stars. The air was filled with an oily, burning stench. The roof must be on fire! Cassie thought of the girls in her family, the kids she saw every day, the kids who at first had been interchangeable to her in their dirty uniforms. Were they trapped inside their locked rooms, already unconscious from the smoke?

A sob burst from her, and Cassie stumbled, blinded by her own tears. Why had she left Hayley behind? She should have insisted. Maybe they both could have made it. What would Gary do to her now? Would he turn her over to Hector?

Then there was the sound of a vehicle, very near, and Cassie threw herself facedown on the rocky ground. Headlights swept over her. It was a pickup, jouncing its way to the compound from the village. The village lay directly between her and the U.S. When the sun was up, she could use the compass ring on her watch, but not now. For now, she had to put as much distance between herself and Peaceful Cove as she could. She cut to the right, determined to give the village a wide berth.

She ran through a palm grove, then down a slope, holding her arms outstretched in front of her to keep from running into something. With one hand she still gripped the snorkel, with the other her flippers. The wet backpack thumped against her spine.

Gradually, Cassie's eyes adjusted to the dark. Things were shadows upon shadows. At one point she dug a hole for her snorkel gear, using the stiff tube of the snorkel itself instead of her bare hands. She'd heard that tarantulas like to bury themselves in the sand, and she didn't want to grab one. Afterward, she kicked the sand over. It made a little mound, but in the dark, it looked good enough to be missed for a day or two.

She sat on the ground, took off her Nikes, then pulled on her jeans over legs that already stung from a dozen nicks and cuts. As she put on socks and then her shoes again, Cassie took stock of what she had. One Powerbar, eleven $20 bills, a watch with a compass ring that was more like a toy, a half gallon of water, and, if you didn't count swearing, three dozen words in Spanish. She thought of the kid Hayley said had died in the desert, then pushed the thought away.

A ridge rose ahead of her, steep and dark. She saw it by absence more than presence, a shadow that covered the stars. Grabbing at roots and outcroppings, Cassie started climbing, sometimes on her knees. Once she tumbled backward, ending up on her shoulder blades, scratched and panting, her knee next to her shoulder.

When she righted herself, she looked behind her and saw a half dozen flickers far away. Little lights on the move. They looked the way she imagined fireflies might. Only these glimmers, Cassie knew, belonged to flashlights. Flashlights looking for her. She had been thinking about resting, her breath scouring her lungs, but instead she turned and went on, faster than before, half running down the other side of the ridge.

She walked for hours. The clouds had cleared and the moon helped her with its silvery-blue light. She had put on her sweater, but still she could not stop shaking, her chattering teeth the only sound. She passed through ranchland where a half dozen scrawny cows slept, standing stock-still. A coyote yipped in the distance.

Finally, the edge of the sky began to lighten. When the sun rose, she followed Hayley's directions and pointed the hour hand of her watch at it, then rotated the compass directional ring until the S was past the hour hand, halfway between it and the 12. She looked back down at her watch again, lined herself up so that she was facing north. Had she been walking in the right direction all night? Cassie was afraid her direction had been more northeast, but she wasn't sure. She hoped that she wasn't too far away from San Diego.

She wanted desperately to stop, to curl up someplace and sleep, but she knew she had to keep on. A cactus beckoned her, looking like something out of a Road Runner cartoon, as tall as a man, complete with arms. The more distance she put between herself and Peaceful Cove, the better. A few people with pickups and binoculars could make short work of searching for her. From her backpack, she pulled out her sunscreen, smeared some on, then pulled on a baseball cap to shade her eyes. Taking out her water bottle, she let herself take two sips. She had to make it last.

Cassie kept on, threading her way through squat barrel cacti with their thick, sharp spines, and cholla cacti with their fine, silvery ones. The back of her heels felt hot. Blisters were forming where no shoes had rubbed for weeks. A cottontail rabbit bounded away from her into the brush, its white tail winking. Every now and then Cassie would come across evidence that people had passed this way before, and these seemed like a good sign. An opened sardine can, a crumpled tube of Mexican toothpaste, an empty white plastic water jug caught up in the brush.

Every hour, she adjusted her watch to make sure she was moving north. By midafternoon she stood on the crest of a long fold of a mountain. Shading her eyes, Cassie spent a long time looking behind her. She saw nothing moving, no people, no plumes of dust trailed by cars. But instead of feeling reassured, Cassie felt alone and insignificant, as if at any moment she might disappear. She could get hurt or trapped and slowly die here and no one would ever know. Pushing the thought away, she lay down in the shadow of a rock outcropping and draped her pack over her face. She tried to forget how thirsty she was and sleep.

When she awoke two hours later, Cassie ate half the Powerbar. It was dry and crumbly and it parched her mouth. She took out her water bottle and shook it. Half gone. She had watched more than one kid pass out at Peaceful Cove from the heat, so she knew how important it was to drink enough water, but she also knew once she finished it, there wouldn't be anyplace to get more. She compromised by drinking only a few swallows.

The sun was lower in the sky, but the day was, if anything, hotter. Plus, the air was heavy with moisture, and dark clouds were massing on the southern horizon. The air shimmered and played tricks on her, making the mountains appear to move. A half hour later, a cool, narrow sandstone canyon beckoned her. About thirty feet deep, it ran roughly north, so she clambered down into its shady depths. A small stream trickled over the rocks, and she took off her shoes, knotted the laces around her neck, and waded. The cool water felt good against her blisters. Beneath her feet, the stones were smooth and slippery. She wished she could drink the water, but she knew it was too dangerous.

A drop of rain landed on her cheek, then another on her arm. In the distance she heard the low grumble of thunder. She looked up at the sky. It was all dark gray now, and the light had an odd greenish cast. Sheltered by the canyon, she hadn't noticed that the wind had picked up.

Her eye caught on something she had seen earlier, but not paid attention to. There were branches and sometimes whole logs tangled high up at the edge of the canyon. How had they gotten wedged so far up there? The stream was deeper now than it had been earlier, turbid with silt. More raindrops freckled her arms.

There was a rumbling sound like an approaching freight train. Head cocked, Cassie tried to figure out what it meant. Then she realized that the canyon was acting like a funnel, channeling all the rain that had landed to the south of her. And that meant—

With a burst of energy, she ran toward the side of the canyon. There was no easy way out, just a mad scramble up the side. Ignoring her stubbed toes, she clambered up, her feet and fingers finding crevices and notches, sometimes creating them by sheer force of will.

Halfway up, Cassie turned just in time to see a wall of water thunder into the canyon. Her scream was lost in the roar of the flash flood.

A second later, there was a river rising under her feet. Water lapped at her toes, then sucked at her calves. She scrambled faster, just managing to keep ahead of the water. A passing branch scratched her back. Raindrops stung her arms and face. Nearly at the top, Cassie looked behind her. The little trickling stream now nearly reached the top of the canyon. Filled with broken branches, the water was the color of mud. The cataract was only a few inches below her, so fast it created its own breeze. With a final fevered burst, Cassie grabbed a stone at the lip of the canyon. It came away in her hand, anchoring her to nothing but air.

She fell backward, arms pinwheeling. At the last minute, she reached out and just managed to snag a dangling root. For a long moment, she hung suspended, her shoulder screaming. Then she found another root, and then a toehold, and another, and painfully dragged herself to the top. Panting, she lay on her belly, ignoring the stinging rain.

Lightning flickered down and touched a small wizened tree less than three hundred feet away. The thunder was directly overhead, as loud as artillery. Cassie realized that if she stood up, she would be the tallest thing around, a human lightning rod.

She had to get to shelter. In the flare of another lightning strike, she saw a rock outcropping a few hundred yards away. She ran through standing water, the wind a giant hand at her back. Between the wind and the rain, it was nearly impossible to breathe.

Cassie crouched under the lip of rock, just big enough to shelter her. Rain sheeted from it. It was as if she had crawled under a waterfall. But as quickly as it came, the rush of water began to slow to a trickle, then a few drips. The light changed as the clouds parted. By the time she left her shelter, the sun was dazzling, sparkling off the dozens of puddles, the ground steaming. Water had collected on top of the rock that had sheltered her. She lowered her head and sucked it dry, not even minding the grit it left on her tongue.

She walked for another hour, two, her clothes gradually growing damp, then dry. As the sun was setting, she realized she was staggering. Again, she looked behind her for any signs of pursuit, saw none. Finally she rolled herself into a ball and slept with her back against a rock. Although the air was cool, the stone against her back was warm.

She awoke the next morning, ate the rest of the Powerbar, used her watch to figure out north again, and kept on. Cassie calculated that she'd been walking the better part of twenty-four hours. The blisters on her heels were filled with water, hot and tight, but she tried to ignore the pain.

As the heat began to rise, she found the faint trace of a road. In the brush on either side were dozens of discarded white plastic jugs and shreds of newspaper that had been used as toilet paper. A faded Mexican comic book waved in the breeze. Cassie hoped that all these discards meant she was getting close to the border.

Stumbling through the sand and scrub, she searched in vain for shade. She shook the last few drops of water onto her tongue, then put the empty bottle in her pack. She should have drunk up all the puddles yesterday, but Cassie had been afraid she would get alkali poisoning or something. Now Cassie's mouth was cold and dry, while her face was burning and wet with sweat. Despite the sunscreen she kept reapplying, her face felt like it was cracking when she squinted. She had planned to spend the heat of the day resting in a shadowed cleft, but there was no shade, just desert specked with mesquite shrubs, yuccas, and prickly pear. She kept on.

Just as darkness fell, she crossed a river, holding her shoes and pack above her head. The water was low, no higher than her belly button. Surrendering to temptation, she bent her head to the water and drank a few sips. It tasted like chemicals and left her tongue feeling coated. In the fading light, the river looked more like oil than water. On the far side, the road was tire tracks worn into the dirt, the moon a tiny smudged thumbprint on the horizon. She was exhausted, but afraid that if she closed her eyes, they might not open again.

Finally, an hour after sunrise, Cassie found what she thought was the border. Not a twelve-foot-tall steel barricade illuminated by stadium-style lighting and fortified with motion detectors, but a four-foot-high barbed wire fence, cut in places, that stretched as far as she could see. Along the fence, tiny flags of torn clothing fluttered in the breeze. Turning sideways, Cassie simply walked through. It seemed too easy. And, her brain fuzzily realized, that easiness told her something. This couldn't be a border next to a major metropolitan area. It must be in the middle of nowhere. That first night she must have angled too far east, so now she was nowhere near San Diego.

She was resting in the shadow of a large cactus when she saw a green open-sided Jeep jouncing across the flats. After three days of running, it took Cassie a minute to realize that, now that she was finally in America, a vehicle meant rescue. Water. An adult who would listen to her. Water. Food. Transportation to a flushing toilet and a bed. Water.

As the Jeep got closer, she saw that the two men inside wore uniforms, and there were white logos stenciled on the door panels. The Border Patrol. She stood up, waving her arms.

The Jeep slowed to a stop. Two men in green uniforms jumped out. One of the men pulled a squared-off gun from the holster on his belt. *"¡Manos para arriba!"* He was pointing the gun directly at her chest.

thirty

June 19

"Don't shoot! Don't shoot!" Cassie shouted. Or tried to. Her voice was a strangled whisper, her tongue so swollen, it refused to shape the words.

The man with the gun narrowed his eyes, but kept his weapon trained on Cassie. He was gray-haired, lean, and weather-beaten. The second man, who wore the waistband of his pants below his ample belly, pulled a walkie-talkie from his belt. "Romeo, be advised, we just captured an SBI. Mexican female, age about nineteen. Alone. Over."

The walkie-talkie crackled in return. "Copy that, Foxtrot. Should we come search the arroyo? Over."

"Affirmative your last. Where there's smoke, there's fire. Over and out."

Cassie tried again to moisten her mouth, not moving her eyes from the gun. "Not Mexican. American. Need water."

The one called Foxtrot leaned into the Jeep and handed her a quart bottle of Safeway brand water. Her hands shook so much, it was hard to twist open the cap. Cassie drank until the bottle was empty, closing her eyes. When she opened them again, the man with the gun had lowered it until it was pointing at the ground.

"I'm not Mexican," Cassie repeated, her saliva still thick. "I'm American."

"Then prove it! Show me some ID." Even though he looked as old as Cassie's grandfather, the man with the gun was giddy with excitement. "You're an illegal."

"I am not. I'm just as American as you." She looked past him at the logo stenciled on the Jeep's door panel. An eagle gripping arrows, encircled by the words *National Border Watch*. That didn't sound quite right.

"Then show us some ID."

"I don't have any ID." Cassie scrambled for a cover story. She was far closer to Peaceful Cove than she was to Portland, and she suddenly remembered Father Gary saying that they had custody rights. "I was in Tijuana and some people robbed me and took me out in the desert. They stole my ID. My name's"—she hesitated and hoped they didn't notice—"Carrie Johnson."

"I still say she's a *pollo*," the older man said.

"A chicken?" Cassie felt confused.

The two men exchanged glances. "For an American, you speak pretty good Spanish," the skinny one said. "A pollo's an illegal immigrant."

"You've got to speak some Spanish to live in America today," she said.

"She's got a point there, Davis," Foxtrot said.

"She could still be an SBI who learned her English off TV." But Davis holstered his gun.

"What's an SBI?" Cassie asked, remembering what Foxtrot had said.

"Suspected border intruder. We use that term because we don't know if people are illegals or not," Foxtrot said. "They could be very lost Mexican hikers. Not likely, but still."

"Are you the Border Patrol?"

"The Border Patrol?" Davis snorted. "The Border Patrol is inefficient at best. We're with National Border Watch. NBW. You might have heard of us?"

Cassie shook her head, then felt dizzy and regretted it. Her stomach was as tight as a water balloon.

"This border"—Davis waved his hand in the direction of the fence—"is no border at all. It's like a trapdoor into America. In the last two years, the NBW has captured more than thirty-three hundred illegal immigrants."

"If you're not the Border Patrol, then why do you have guns?"

"They're not guns—they're tasers. They shoot little darts on wires, not bullets. Basically, they just give you a big electric shock," Davis said. "Make it so you can't run away."

"And it's all legal," Foxtrot added.

Davis said, "Let's take you back to the house, check out the bona fides. Foxtrot, you go check the arroyos and cuts, just in case there are any more where she came from." He turned to Cassie. "Go on, get in back."

Wire mesh separated the two seats, reminding Cassie uncomfortably of the van that had taken her to Mexico in the first place. Was she a prisoner again? It took them twenty minutes to drive to Davis's house. It looked like any ranch house in the suburbs of Portland, at least any suburban ranch house surrounded by nothing but desert and barbed wire and with a twenty-foot-tall metal viewing tower next to it.

Inside, the house was clean and quiet. The curtains were all drawn tight, giving the house a muffled and sleepy feel, as if it had just settled down for a long siesta. There was a cream-colored carpet, a blue plaid couch and a matching recliner. There was no art on the walls and nothing out of place. She shivered in the air-conditioning, unaccustomed to feeling cool.

"Diana," Davis called out. He unbuckled his gun belt and put it on a high shelf next to the door, along with his keys. A plump woman appeared in the kitchen doorway and walked toward them, wiping her hands on a white apron.

"This is my wife, Diana. Diana, this is Carrie," Davis said.

She smelled like cookies. The sweet scent cramped Cassie's stomach. She put her hand on the wall to steady herself.

"When did you last eat?" Davis rapped out.

Cassie couldn't even remember anymore. "Two days ago?"

"Don't just stand there, Diana, fix the girl a plate."

Without speaking, Diana turned and hurried back into the kitchen. Davis took Cassie's elbow and led her into the dining room, which had a long wooden table and eight ladder-back chairs. Three little girls crept into the hall and stared at her. The oldest looked about six.

It was only a minute before Diana was back with a glass of milk and a white plate with a cheese sandwich, potato chips, and a pickle.

"Thank you," Cassie mumbled to Diana with her mouth full. "This is really good." Her face was lined but not old. Cassie guessed she was at least thirty years younger than her husband.

Davis pulled out a chair, straddled it. "Tell me again what happened to you."

"Some friends and I went to Tijuana to party. Somebody must have put something in my drink. The next thing I knew, I was wandering around in the desert by myself and my purse was gone."

"Are you even legally old enough to drink, young lady?"

"Well, no, but—"

"And your parents—what did they think about it?"

"They're divorced. And it was fine with my mom."

Cassie nodded her head, which made her feel dizzy. She closed her eyes.

Davis laid a hand on her shoulder. His fingers felt long and spidery. "You look like you could use a nap. I'll have Diana put you in the guest room."

thirty-one

June 20

At one in the morning, Cassie was driving the Jeep down a deserted road. On the seat beside her was Davis's taser and holster. With luck, she might have a five-hour head start. Or less. Davis looked like the kind of guy who would get up early.

When she had woken from her nap, she had gotten up and started to go down the hall. Then she heard Diana and Davis talking. Suspicious of her story, they thought she was a runaway, and hoped there was a reward. They were planning on turning her over to the cops the next day. Cassie wasn't sure what the cops would do—but she didn't want to take the slightest chance they would send her back to Peaceful Cove. She decided she had to cut and run while they still thought her too worn-out from her ordeal to think for herself. She didn't have to feign exhaustion at the dinner table, and it took all her energy to stay awake until they went to bed. When she reached for the keys on the shelf Davis had left them on, her fingers touched something else. The holster for the taser. She decided to take it as well. If Davis did come hunting her, now he couldn't come armed.

At first her hands were slick on the wheel. Cassie had never driven by herself before, but the road was just a flat place in the middle of a bigger flat place. She slowly lost her fear and grew nearly comfortable. An hour later, she merged onto another road heading north. Later, she turned onto an even bigger road, then finally to a freeway. At five in the morning, the sky just getting light, she pulled into a rest area. She parked the car next to the restroom and put the keys under the mat. Buckling the taser's holster around her waist, she tied a huge sweatshirt of Diana's over it, then got out and locked the door.

Over the next hour, several cars with Oregon or Washington plates drove into the rest stop. Cassie rejected the first one, a man driving alone (would-be rapist), then the second, a woman who looked about fifty (more likely to insist on phoning her mom and Rick), and finally the third car, which held a couple (twice as many questions). She felt jumpy as her head start slowly evaporated, but she didn't want to end up with the wrong rescuer twice. Finally, she saw a young woman driving a fifteen-year-old Toyota with Oregon plates pull in to the rest stop. As the woman bought a Diet Coke from a vending machine, Cassie walked over to her. She was slender and wore jeans, Birkenstocks, and a sleeveless shirt without benefit of a bra.

"You're from Oregon?"

"Yeah." The woman looked at her curiously. She lifted her blond hair from her shoulders and rested the cold can on the back of her neck. Even though it was still early in the morning, the day was already hot.

"I'm from Portland."

"Oh, really?" The woman smiled now. In Portland she might not have talked to Cassie, but now that they were far from home, it was like they were old friends. "From what part?"

"West Hills."

"I live in Multnomah Village!" The two areas of the city were only a few miles apart.

"Are you going back to Portland now? Can you maybe give me a ride?"

The smile left her face and the other woman looked Cassie up and down. "How come you can't just get back the way you came?"

"I met this guy, see, but it didn't work out. He talked me into coming with him, but he wanted more than I wanted to give him. So he kicked me out of the car and took off." Cassie was getting better at spinning alibis.

"That jerk! But what about your parents? Shouldn't we call them? They must be worried about you."

Cassie figured the "we" was a good sign. "If I do, I'm afraid they'll just call the cops and try to have me picked up. My stepdad is pretty hardcore. I want to talk to them face-to-face to get this whole thing straightened out." Cassie played her trump card, the other reason she had waited until she spotted a young-looking driver driving a beat-up old car. "Besides, I can pay you. At least the jerk left me my babysitting money."

thirty-two

June 21

Thatcher's house was dark. Cassie counted windows twice before she was sure she was standing outside his bedroom, then rapped lightly. The sound seemed as loud as a pistol shot.

She listened closely, but heard nothing. After counting to thirty, she knocked again. The curtain was pushed back, and there was Thatcher, his hair tangled from sleep, looking younger—too young, really, to help her. Why was she here? Then Cassie remembered that she didn't have anyplace else to go.

Thatcher's mouth fell open. Fumbling with the lock, he finally managed to slide the window up. His voice was a piercing whisper.

"Cassie? Cassie! I thought you were dead." His face was pale, his eyes wide. Cassie realized she was used to the blank expression kids quickly assumed at Peaceful Cove. As she looked at Thatcher's open face, tears pricked Cassie's eyes. She found she couldn't speak. Leaning down, he gathered her cold hands in his warm ones. "Do you think you could climb in?"

She put her hands on the sill, levered herself up, managed to get one leg over. She lost her balance and tumbled forward onto Thatcher's bed. The nest of covers was still warm from his body.

He pulled her up to a sitting position, then yanked the covers up around his waist when he realized he was only wearing boxers.

Reaching forward, he took her hands again. She noticed that he was shaking. "I can't believe it's you."

"Why did you think I was dead?"

"The article said you were missing and probably dead."

"What article?"

"An article from a newspaper that I found online. It wasn't even in the *Oregonian*. After your mom told me that they had sent you to that school, I was searching Google every day, looking for information about Peaceful Cove. And then I saw the article about the fire."

"Can you show me?" Cassie asked.

He tapped the space bar on his Macintosh and it came to life. "I bookmarked it," he said as he pulled up the article. She scrolled past an explanation of how Peaceful Cove worked, slowing when she came to the description of the fire:

With many interior doors locked and windows barred, it was difficult for students to find a way out. Dozens of students suffered from smoke inhalation and burns, most of them minor. Once the teens managed to leave the smoky building and gather in the courtyard, according to eyewitness reports, they began to rebel, staging a small-scale riot. The gate was forced open. Under the cover of darkness, teens ran for the nearby village, in the direction of the beach, or out into the desert. Some staff members tried to restrain the children by dragging them back inside the compound, beating them with fists and sticks, and, some assert, threatening them with guns. Local authorities later intervened and arranged for the students to be returned to their parents in the United States.

Two sixteen-year-old American students, Hayley Hedges and Cassie Streng, are missing. There is evidence they may have tried to escape the flames by climbing a fence next to a steep cliff overlooking the ocean. Authorities say that if so, their bodies may never be recovered.

In Mexico, Gary Fisk was detained on Thursday night on a local prosecutor's complaints of physical and psychological abuse. Police, who seized the program's computers and files, said that Fisk himself appeared to have sustained injuries in a beating administered by his former students during the riot.

Cassie's chest felt bound by an iron band. Hayley must be dead.

Thatcher and Cassie both jumped when the door flew open to reveal a woman with dark, tousled hair.

"I guess I should be glad she still has her clothes on, Thatch." Her voice was a low rasp.

"Mom!" He and Cassie drew apart and got to their feet. "This is my friend Cassie, the one I told you about. Cassie, this is my mom, Lori."

"You mean the one you cried your eyes out over? I'm so glad you're alive—but why are you here, Cassie?" Lori's words were blunt, but her expression had softened. "Your mom's crazy with worry."

"We saw her at the store yesterday," Thatcher said.

Cassie's heart felt squeezed. "How did she look? Has she had the baby yet?"

Lori looked at her steadily. "They took her off bed rest, but she hasn't had the baby yet. And she looks exhausted. They won't let her travel to Mexico until she's had the baby. She said as soon as she does, she's going down there to find you. Only she's worried it will just be your body. You need to go to her."

Cassie felt like she was being torn apart. "I want to see my mom so bad, but once my stepfather knows I'm alive, I'll be gone again.

Someplace even farther away than Mexico. Rick's pretty serious about making sure I don't talk about, about . . ."

Lori finished Cassie's sentence for her. "About the Socom, right?"

Cassie looked at Thatcher. "You told her?"

"I had to explain why I was so upset when you didn't show up at school. After a week I went to your house and talked to your mom. She told me Rick had found crystal meth in your room."

The injustice of it burned Cassie afresh. "How can she believe that!"

Thatcher looked away. "I don't know that she does. I told her I didn't believe it, and she looked away and didn't say anything."

Cassie looked at Lori. "Do you believe us? I mean, about me not using drugs and my stepfather giving them to kids?"

Lori ran her hand through her hair so that it stood up in a wild halo around her head. "To be honest, I don't know what to believe. You seem like a good kid. And I know Thatch likes you and trusts you." She sighed. "Thatch told me how much money your stepfather gets for every kid enrolled in the drug study. With that kind of money at stake, people do bad things."

Cassie let herself relax a little. It didn't sound as if Lori was going to call her mom or the police—at least not right away. She yawned, a yawn that went on and on until she actually staggered.

"Come on, kids," Lori said. "How about if I make us some cocoa?"

"It's almost time to get up anyway, Mom. Maybe you should make it coffee."

Cassie saw that what Thatcher said was true. The sky was growing light. She looked at her watch. It was a little after five.

She followed Lori out of the room. Behind her she heard Thatcher hopping on one foot as he yanked on a pair of pants.

Watching his mom fill the kettle with water, Cassie started yawning again and couldn't stop.

"You look like you need to go to bed for a week."

"I'm pretty . . . um . . ." Cassie yawned again. "Tired."

"She could sleep here while we're both at work, Mom," Thatcher suggested as he came into the kitchen.

Lori nodded. "Of course she can sleep here. She looks like hell. But she should stay inside until we come home. Her folks live less than two miles away—and there are plenty of kids in this neighborhood who go to West Portland and might recognize her. And after work we can talk about what we are going to do next."

We. Cassie liked the sound of that. She was safe now, safe for the first time in months.

"So you're working now, Thatcher?"

"I'm working with Mom at Goodwill. Want us to bring you back a Crock-Pot or a plastic lei?"

"No, thanks. I'm good." She took the thick white mug of cocoa Lori handed her, before Lori poured coffee for herself and Thatcher. They sat down at the dining room table and she told them about Peaceful Cove and how she had escaped.

Lori leaned forward. "Don't you think if you told your mother all this that she would believe you?"

Cassie hesitated. "I honestly don't know. We used to be pretty close, but now she only listens to Rick. I'm thinking of going to my dad now that I can tell him what was really going on, but he doesn't have custody and he lives in Minor. And he doesn't have the money to go to court to fight for custody."

Lori sighed. "I don't feel right about not telling your mom you're back. This is killing her."

Tears started to run down Cassie's face. "But if I tell her, she'll tell Rick, and then I'll be off in another school I won't be able to escape from."

"Just for today, Mom," Thatcher said. "Let Cassie get some sleep, and then tonight we can figure out what to do."

Before she left for work, Lori gave Cassie a hug. Even though she was the wrong height and didn't smell anything like Jackie, Cassie choked with tears again. Lori felt like a mom.

thirty-three

June 23

Standing in her old living room, Cassie took a deep breath. She could feel her pulse in her throat. The big house felt oddly hollow and fake, like a stage set or a museum diorama, rather than someplace people lived.

At 7:00 A.M., she and Thatcher had staked out the house, parking his mom's car a block away. Today was Lori's day off, and she was still asleep. They knew she wouldn't approve of what they were doing, so they hadn't told her. Rick had left the house at 7:40, the same time he always had when Cassie lived with them. Seeing him pass by in his BMW, his expression concealed by his expensive sunglasses, Cassie found her fists clenching. Did he ever think about her, feel remorse for his lies? Did he ever doubt that he had done the right thing by putting Ben, Carmen, and Darren on Socom?

The next hour dragged by. With no job, Jackie didn't have a set routine, but Cassie knew she liked to get her errands done first thing in the morning. Finally, they saw the garage door rise and her car back out of the driveway. It turned the other way, so Cassie was spared the sight of her mother's face. But even watching the black dot of her head made Cassie's throat close with tears.

"Ready?" Thatcher asked. Then he saw her face and patted her knee. "Oh, Cas, I'm sorry."

She took a deep, shuddering breath, trying to focus as she repeated their plan one more time. "Okay, if you see anybody, honk the horn three times. Then I'll reset the security alarm, go out the back door and over the fence. I'll meet you at the tennis courts two blocks from here. If I don't come in thirty minutes, call the police."

Thatcher sat quietly through her recitation, even though he had heard it a dozen times already. He patted her knee again. "Good luck."

Cassie walked as fast as she dared up the street, through the side yard, and into the back. Reaching under the deck, she found the hook her mother had hung an extra key on. An extra key Rick knew nothing about.

But there was still the alarm. She put the key in the door, opened it, and the alarm began to beep a warning. Cassie punched in the security code. It beeped twice and then fell silent. Good. They hadn't changed the code. She stood still for a second, just breathing.

Then she shook herself. She had to find proof about what Rick was doing—and quickly. She tried the handle to his office. Locked. According to the plan, Cassie should now be shimming it open, even taking it off its hinges if necessary, but she was suddenly overcome by exhaustion. Even if she did manage to get in, there was no guarantee she would find anything on his computer or in his files that spelled out the problems with Socom. Rick had had plenty of time to change everything.

She found herself walking up the stairs to her room. Everything was the way she had left it, except for her bed. It was unmade, as it had been when Cassie had left for school the day she was kidnapped, but the pillow was now wadded up and surrounded by a dozen crumpled tissues. She imagined her mother lying on the bed, weeping.

The closet was stuffed full of clothes. It was hard to believe she had gone from having so much to being able to keep everything she owned in a plastic milk crate—with room to spare. The only thing Cassie took was an old pair of sneakers from the back of the closet. The Nikes she had worn in the desert were coming unstitched at the toes.

Back downstairs, she started to force herself to search the kitchen junk drawer for a screwdriver. Her eye was caught by a checklist on the counter, written in Rick's distinctive handwriting.

Call Food in Bloom, review menu – order more shrimp?
Pick up glasses
Make sure servers know to wear black and white
Get extra Socom brochures from printer
Make sure Infocus machine is working for presentation

Next to the list was a cream-colored invitation. *Please join us for a reception followed by an opportunity to learn more about Socom. This is your chance to learn more about the answer for troubled adolescents, as well as how to get in at the "ground floor" of a pre-IPO enterprise.* Cassie looked at the date. The party was being held on Saturday— two days from now.

Outside, a horn honked three times. Cassie jumped, her heart pounding.

Shoes in hand, Cassie snatched up the extra key, hit the exit button on the alarm, and then went out the back door. But instead of scrambling for the fence, she hid behind the big cedar, watching the kitchen window. In a few minutes, her mother came in. At this distance it was hard to see her clearly, but her face seemed pale and thin. She opened and closed cupboard doors, obviously putting groceries away. Cassie wanted nothing so much as to run back to the house and into her mother's arms. Instead she turned away and climbed over the neighbor's fence. Two months ago, climbing a six-foot-tall fence would have seemed a major obstacle. Now it was barely worth noting.

When Thatcher saw her walking toward the tennis courts, he ran to her and pulled her into his arms. Cassie felt beyond tears.

She told him what had happened. "I've got nothing, Thatcher. Nothing. There's no way we can prove he's connected to these deaths."

"I wouldn't be so sure about that," he said slowly. "There might just be a way."

thirty-four

June 25

Cassie smiled shyly at Thatcher. He ducked his head, but not before smiling back. She had never gone to a prom, but she imagined it must feel something like this. Both of them dressed like grown-ups, trying out new selves for a night. Yesterday, Lori had brought home outfits from Goodwill. For Thatcher, it was a white dress shirt, now freshly pressed, and black gabardine dress pants. His hair had been slicked back into a ponytail, and his piercings were gone.

Cassie was a blonde now. Thatcher had taken to calling her "Inga, the Swedish model," and even though she protested, it made Cassie flush with an odd pleasure. When she looked in the mirror, between the new hair color and the twenty pounds she had lost at Peaceful Cove, she didn't recognize herself—and she hoped Rick wouldn't, either.

For Cassie, Lori had brought home a loose white peasant blouse with a red drawstring and a black velvet skirt that came just above her knees. She had even found some size ten black sandals with two-inch heels.

Cars lined both sides of the street, and they had to park three blocks away. Cassie led Lori and Thatcher to the back door. Under his arm, Thatcher carried the materials they had spent the day at

Kinko's producing. As they had hoped, the kitchen was a swirl of activity, with a dozen staff dressed in black and white rinsing glasses, prepping food, and coming and going with silver trays. No one looked at them twice. Cassie thought they were probably used to working with crews that changed for every event.

She stashed the Kinko's bag in the mudroom. Thatcher picked up a serving platter filled with crab puffs. "I'll go see if the reporter is here," he told Cassie before walking out into the great room.

He was back in thirty seconds. "Michelle's here, all right. Standing right next to Rick and asking him lots of questions." Thatcher had called the reporter two days earlier and told her about Cassie and Peaceful Cove, as well as the party, saying, "You get in and we'll promise you a show." Now they just had to deliver.

Lori wheeled up a metal cart draped in white. It held a few dirty glasses. "Trade me," she said to Thatcher, then took his tray of canapés and disappeared. Cassie got the Kinko's bag and put it on the lower level of the cart. She took a deep breath. It was now or never. The longer she hung out in the kitchen, the more likely that they would be found out, by her mom or Rick or even the real catering staff. "It's showtime," she said to Thatcher.

The room was crowded with close to a hundred people sipping drinks, nibbling shrimp, and listening to Rick, who stood at the front of the room, gesturing.

"The adolescent brain is still maturing. It's why teenagers are so much more likely to engage in risky behavior. Many teenagers lack certain brain chemicals that allow them to make mature judgments or even regulate their own emotions. But Socom provides that missing piece. When we take this company public, we fully expect to gain at least forty percent of the existing market share for adolescent depression, in addition to opening up new markets. Even given the existing patient profile, this a twelve billion dollar industry." He hit hard on the "b" in billion, and a man standing near Cassie whistled. Smiling, Rick added, "Socom's innovative technology creates an opportunity to obtain and hold a dominant position in the market. Tonight we are offering a pre-IPO opportunity, meaning that you, my friends and colleagues, have the chance to get in on the ground floor before Socom goes public." He clasped his hands. "Now, does anyone have any questions?"

"Dr. Wheeler!" Cassie called out before anyone else could say anything. "Dr. Wheeler, I have a question. Isn't it true that Socom causes delusions that have led to the deaths of three teens?"

"That's—that's not true," Rick stammered. "With all drugs that treat depression, of course there is a small but recognized risk that as the patient's depression and inertia begin to lift, they may actually be at slightly greater risk for suicidal ideation. But that risk is no greater for patients taking Socom than for any other drug."

Cassie soldiered on, making an effort to match his crisp tone and matter-of-fact delivery. "But we're not talking about suicidal thoughts, are we, Dr. Wheeler? We are talking about kids who had become so delusional, they couldn't tell what was real and what were their demons. Kids like Darren Cartwright. Ben Tranbarger. Carmen Hernandez." As Cassie said each name, Thatcher reached under the tablecloth on the serving cart to hand her a blown-up photo scanned from the yearbook and mounted on foam core. She lined them up on top of the grand piano. There were murmurs now. "All patients of yours. All kids you prescribed Socom to. For them, Socom ultimately led to their suicides."

"That's conjecture!" Rick said quickly, his voice too loud in the now-hushed room. "You've got no proof."

"But we do have proof, Dr. Wheeler," Thatcher said, his voice giving the word *doctor* a sarcastic spin. "Look at the signatures on these permission forms. It's clear all of them were signed by the same person. And that person was you. You forged the permissions from these teens' parents. They never knew you were injecting their children with an experimental drug." Three more pieces of foam core, all showing a Socom consent form, all showing spiky, illegible signatures that slanted to the left. After Cassie had been unable to get the files from the house, Thatcher had taken his computer to his part-time job and thrown himself on the mercy of his buddies in technical support. One of them had managed to resurrect the file.

"Where did you get those?" Rick demanded. "Those are private records. Besides, those three only represent a small, small percentage. Less than one in a thousand. For the other 99.9 percent, Socom is a wonder drug. Parents get back their teens the way they used to be. Obedient, polite, well-spoken."

Cassie interrupted. "And sometimes suicidal! Three kids died! Is anything worth that risk?"

Rick shook his head in exaggerated sorrow, his eyes drilling into hers, and Cassie realized he had finally recognized her. "Cassie, Cassie, Cassie. So you've come home. First you act out, and then you use drugs, and then you start a fire at your boarding school that injures dozens of kids." He looked at the crowd. "This is my stepdaughter, folks. She couldn't handle that her mom got remarried, so now she's making up outrageous lies."

"She's telling the truth." People's heads turned to the woman who stood in the hall. With each word, Jackie took a step toward Rick. She was dressed all in black, her face hollow. Her belly jutted so far forward, she had to lean back to counterbalance it. "You tried to tell me that it was a coincidence that Darren was taking Socom. You said Ben was never on it. And I never even knew about

Carmen." Jackie now stood directly in front of him, her hands fisted on her hips. "Now I know you lied."

Michelle was the first in the crowd to move. Holding a silver tape recorder, she walked up to Rick and held out a tiny microphone toward him. "Michelle Haynes from the *Oregonian*. Would you care to comment on these very serious allegations, Doctor?"

For a moment no one spoke, then there was a sudden swell of voices. "Is this true?" one man called out. "My daughter knew that boy, Ben," another man said, gesturing to Ben's photo, his face drained of color. People turned to each other to ask questions, and many of them turned to Rick. The babble of voices swelled until it became a cacophony.

Rick looked at them all wildly, then suddenly he turned and ran for the front door. He threw it open and ran outside, not even bothering to close it.

Cassie ran after him. The garage door was already half up. Rick was pointing his key fob at his BMW. It chirped in answer. He ducked under the garage door. As he threw open the car door, Cassie reached under her blouse, pulled the taser from her waist pack, and pointed it at him.

Rick was half turned toward her. He managed a laugh, and she realized he thought she was holding a gun. "You would never use that."

"It's easy," Cassie answered. "Just point and shoot."

And she did.

thirty-five

June 27

From the OREGONIAN

Doctor linked to teen deaths

A prominent Southwest Portland psychiatrist was arrested on June 25th, charged with manslaughter and fraud. Richard Wheeler, M.D., specialized in treating adolescents with behavioral issues.

As a psychiatrist, Wheeler was licensed to write prescriptions as well as to counsel troubled individuals. He was approached by Socom to enroll patients in a clinical trial of the drug. For every patient he enrolled, he would get $10,000. For many teenagers, Socom seems to have helped them concentrate in school, evened out their mood swings, and relieved the surliness and withdrawal that often go hand-in-hand with puberty. But for some, it also caused delusions. And at least three of those teens committed suicide—deaths that were never reported to the FDA, as mandated by law.

• Ben Tranbarger, 17, drank silver cleaner. Unknown to Ben's mother, Wheeler had enrolled Ben in the Socom study. But five weeks later, Ben began to obsess about being

dirty, showering for hours and taking multiple doses of lax-
atives. After drinking silver cleaner, he slipped into a coma
and was pronounced dead three days later.

*   • Darren Cartwright, 15. Worried about his depression*
and shyness, his mother took him to see Wheeler. On
Socom, Darren began to believe that he could fly. He died
when he jumped off a seven-story building.

*   • Carmen Hernandez, 16. A high school dropout, Car-*
men was interested when other kids said she could earn
money by enrolling in the study. On Socom, she believed she
was pregnant by Satan, and stabbed herself in the abdomen.
In an interview, the coroner said that while Carmen's in-
juries were definitely self-inflicted, he had never seen any-
thing like them in his 30-year career.

*   Medical ethicist Renee Mestad said, "When you take*
the potential to make a whole lot of money, and add in the
ethical dilemma of whether a person with mental health
issues can even give informed consent, it can really go
wrong." Pending the outcome of the criminal investigation,
Wheeler's medical license has been suspended by Oregon's
board of medical directors.

*   Megan Fuller, a spokesman for Socom, said, "We have*
an extensive system of checks and balances. We are helping
to set industry standards. Even with all that, we didn't un-
cover the fraud."

thirty-six

July 27

The wailing started as Cassie rooted through a cabinet filled with expensive appliances, trying to find the few things that didn't belong to Rick.

"Mom! The baby's crying," Cassie shouted. No answer. The wailing got louder. As she went upstairs, Cassie heard the rush of the shower from the master suite. With four showerheads, it was a place you could lose yourself in blasts of water so loud that not even a one-month-old baby's cries could penetrate.

On tiptoe, as if Noah were asleep instead of screaming his head off, Cassie went into the nursery. She leaned over the bassinet, wincing a little when she saw his face, so red it was nearly purple.

"It's okay," she said. In answer, the corners of the baby's mouth turned down even farther and his mouth opened wider. He was wearing only a onesie, his bare legs kicking. Gingerly, Cassie picked him up, remembering to support his head. It was the first time she had held Noah without someone else watching her.

Jackie had gone into labor the night of the Socom party. Her water broke as Thatcher and Cassie tied Rick up with dishcloths and a half dozen guests called the police on their cell phones. Some had thought Rick was the bad guy, others Cassie. But by the time the cops showed up, Cassie was halfway to the hospital, with

Lori at the wheel of the car and Jackie in the backseat, her feet pressed against the side window while Lori and Cassie yelled at her not to push. Twenty minutes after they'd arrived at the hospital, Noah had been born.

The police, the courts, and the FDA were still sorting everything out, as was Jackie. She was beginning the process of annulment, which Cassie hadn't realized was possible when a marriage had already produced a baby. But an annulment would make it easier if Jackie needed to testify in one of the numerous criminal and civil lawsuits being filed against Rick and Socom. Although her testimony might not be needed. Late last week had come word that Rick had decided to cooperate with the authorities.

Cassie tucked Noah's head under her chin and patted him on the back. The decibel level dropped, but the crying didn't stop. She bounced up and down on her toes, and Noah's cries began to slow. Jiggling even faster, she patted his back more vigorously and was rewarded with a giant burp that a fifty-year-old couch potato would have been proud of. It was so deep and loud that it made Cassie laugh.

The front doorbell rang, and Cassie went downstairs to answer it. It was Thatcher. Lori stood in the driveway, folding down the backseat of her car.

"Hey, little guy," Thatcher said softly, stepping behind Cassie so he could look at the baby's face. His voice changed. "Um, did you know you have spit-up all down your back?"

"Yuck! I'll change when my mom gets done with her shower."

"Mom and I are ready to take another load. How many more boxes do you have?"

"Not too many. We're only taking what we brought, and we didn't have that much to begin with." Cassie smiled. It felt like she was casting off a husk that she didn't need anymore—this house, the furniture, the twin BMWs in the garage. They had next to nothing, but she had never felt richer. One of the few good things Cassie had learned at Peaceful Cove was that she could live without a lot of things. If you had freedom and people you loved, well, that was more than most of the kids at Peaceful Cove had had.

The only other thing she had taken away from Peaceful Cove was her friendship with Hayley. Hayley had originally given the Mexican hospital a false name. She hadn't admitted who she really was until she was sure that the school was going to stay closed. The second-degree burns on her feet and calves were slowly healing. Jackie had tracked her down after finding out from Cassie's dad that Hayley had been her best friend at the school. She had hoped that Hayley might know where Cassie was. When she couldn't locate Hayley's mom right away, Jackie had paid for Hayley to be flown up to Portland for treatment. Actually, Rick had paid for it, even if he hadn't known it. There had been many long discussions since with Hayley's mom, and it looked like Hayley might end up staying in Portland.

Lori came over to them. "I picked up some more stuff for Noah yesterday. A Baby Bjorn that looked like it had never been used." Lori had made it her mission to find the stuff at Goodwill that Jackie and Cassie needed to start their life over again in Portland. Minor held too many memories, and for Jackie, too much guilt.

"I should have asked more questions," Jackie had told Cassie. "I wondered about some of the things that were going on in the office, but I figured I just didn't understand the way things worked. It took me a long time to see that was exactly why Rick hired me—because I didn't know enough to be suspicious. And when I finally

did ask questions, he distracted me by showering me with attention. No one had acted like that toward me for a long time. You
may find this hard to believe, but Rick can be very charming when
he wants to."

Cassie hadn't been able to let it go so easily. Not after everything she had been through. "But you must have known something. All those kids who died in Minor."

"I knew that Darren was on Socom," Jackie had admitted. "I'd
seen him in the office myself. When Darren died, I went to Rick
and said I was concerned. He told me Darren had already had suicidal tendencies. A few weeks later I found out I was pregnant and
Rick told me he wanted to get married and for me to quit working.
Ben died right after that. I asked if he had been on Socom, and
Rick told me he hadn't. He seemed so broken up over Ben's death,
I thought he was telling the truth. And I never even knew that that
girl, Carmen, had been one of Rick's patients." Jackie had sighed.
"I guess I wanted someone who would tell me what to do. Do you
think thirty-nine is too old to try to grow up?"

"What's the alternative?" Cassie had said.

Now Jackie came up behind them, towel-drying her hair.
"Sorry, I didn't even hear him." She reached out and took Noah.
"Did you know that you have spit-up all down your back?" She
walked back into the house.

Thatcher exchanged a smile with Cassie and then said, "I found
something today at Goodwill to replace something you had to
leave down in Mexico."

"What is it?" Cassie asked. She couldn't think of anything she
missed about Peaceful Cove.

He went to the car and came back with his hands behind
his back.

When Cassie saw what was in the mesh bag, she started to

laugh. "I don't think I'm going to need a snorkel set again. At least not for a long, long time."

And then, while they were still both laughing, and before she could think twice about it, Cassie stood on tiptoe and gave Thatcher a kiss.